"Our Author draws you into a diabolical conspiracy—a 'plot' of sorts, to kill a quixotic fabulist known as Ovid (a fool who must go on a road trip, avoiding his doom by hiding from such a call for his assassination). I might point out, in passing, that "Ovid" is an anagram for a "Void" (a kind of hollow, full of missing, ghostly allusions that haunt this story throughout). Our Author has, alas, shown his authorial tradition no sympathy, choosing to draft a book that abandons a common symbol, a minor glyph, which most narrators find crucial in any production of a drama. You can always try your hand at such a task in a roundabout way, but why not scan this book first, so as to fathom how a virtuoso might do it with whimsy."

—Christian Bok, author of *Eunoia*

"In Roundabout, words drift and bob and flow so smoothly that what's missing isn't known. In fact, its omission is the vigor that thrusts it on, its 'limitation' its gift to us all. By plucking a symbol away, playfulness is put on full display, giving us a magical and wondrous work. Book buyers watch out: amazing things await."

—BJ Hollars, author of *Sightings*

T0133292

ROUNDABOUT

An Improvisational Fiction

by Phong

Moon City Press

MOON CITY PRESS
Department of English
Missouri State University
901 South National Avenue
Springfield, Missouri 65897

No part of this book may be reproduced in any form or by any elec-
tronic or mechanical means, including information storage and
retrieval systems, without permission in writing from the publisher,
except in the case of short passages quoted in reviews.

The narratives contained herein are works of fiction. All incidents, situations, institutions, governments, and people are fictional, and any
similarity to characters or persons living or dead is strictly coincidental.

First Edition
Copyright © 2020 by Phong Nguyen
All rights reserved.
Published by Moon City Press, Springfield, Missouri, USA, in 2019.

Library of Congress Cataloging-in-Publication Data

2019953311

Nguyen, Phong
Roundabout/Nguyen, Phong: 1978–

Further Library of Congress information is available upon request.

ISBN-10: 0-913785-41-6
ISBN-13: 978-0-913785-41-6

Cover and illustrations by Sarah Nguyen
Designed by Charli Barnes
Edited by Karen Craigo

Manufactured in the United States of America.

www.mooncitypress.com

Boys throw rocks at frogs in sport, but frogs
do not croak in sport, but with passion.

—*Biont*

ROUNDABOUT

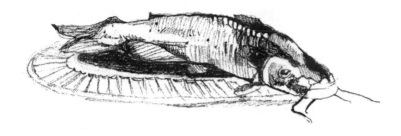

First Part

Ovid Dullann was a promising child who would always stay a promising child—a prodigy grown old and sad. Grow as Ovid might, with him it was always a similar thing in dissimilar proportion, as a truck gradually grows in sound on its approach. As a child in London, Ovid would sit for hours and do drawings of cowboys, worthy of a postcard; as a man living in Wisconsin, Ovid would throw away his Sundays painting portraits of British politicians, both Whig and Tory. If in his childhood Ovid would play mini-golf at an occasional birthday party, in his adulthood Ovid took up golf as a way of blowing off work. Practicing piano at four was now playing piano skillfully, but with no soul, at almost fifty.

For all his prodigious output as a child, as an adult Ovid did not stand out in any of his strivings. Ovid would not rock any boats, and most of all, would not allow any stain of doubt to soil his shining narcissism. A film fanatic and an aspiring visual artist, a musician, an author, an historian, and an arm-chair political analyst, having a child or two of his own still could not disarm his youthful fascination with watching flicks, jamming out on guitar, flipping through a thick biography or two, and making art of any kind. Nobody could. But his natural curiosity took a turn toward compulsion at his forty-ninth birthday party.

It was April first of 2004. Ovid was actually born on April Fool's Day, and that is just to start with: All of Ovid's days would rapidly turn into fool's days.

His missus, Anna, was cooking up a catfish—Ovid's annual birthday dish. Ovid always had an affinity for catfish—*cat-fish*, who must carry on in this binary world as both cat and fish, without knowing which animal it truly is (but, as with Carroll's Walrus, this sympathy for Ovid's food did not stop him from consuming it).

On this occasion, Ovid and his two kids—a boy and a girl—sat around in plush Victorian armchairs, finishing off bits of catfish and looking forward to what was coming up: a custard fruit tart with apricot and plum, a sprig of mint, and a marzipan crust. So Anna brought out Ovid's birthday tart, firing it up with a match and singing, "Happy birthday to you. Happy birthday to you. Happy birthday to Ovid. Happy birthday to you!" to which Ovid's brood mumblingly sang along.

But as soon as this tart was through—producing an aluminum tin without a crumb in it—Ovid's family ran off to do solitary things, as though finally through with an obnoxious obligation.

Ovid and Anna had twins: His boy was Aaron; his girl, Alyssa. Aaron was a smart kid, full of cunning pranks, such as filling his dad's Toyota with packing Styrofoam, or programming Alyssa's iPod to play only soft rock, or crank-calling his mom and acting out a highly wrought drama in which Alyssa is stuck in prison. All of it was in good humor, but for a singular anomaly: On January first of 2000 (in a fit of Y2K mania), whilst trying to blow up a toy robot with an M-60, Aaron lit up his dad's porch with a stray spark, and Ovid could hardly contain this conflagration with his foam spray. Naturally, Ovid's first priority was to confirm that his son was OK, but it struck him as odd that Aaron could not stop smiling as a glowing pit of ash was forming in that spot upon which his porch had, until now, stood. (Now halfway to thirty, Aaron is still fond of lighting a match on occasion.)

Though officially a child, Aaron had a surprising physical maturity that, in many situations, would allow him to pass as an adult. In fact, Aaron was planning on going to a strip club that night ("passing" as an "adult"), but Ovid caught him on his way out and told him to go to his room. Aaron sulkily slunk upstairs. Though it was Ovid's birthday, Aaron had his own party plans. (Alyssa was also going to a strip club that night, though Ovid was not as suspicious of Alyssa—his darling "baby girl"—so did nothing to thwart it.)

Alyssa was as curious as Aaron, but so kind and matronly that it could trick you into dropping your guard. But Alyssa's way of acting kind was dodgy, as if this joy was only a front for a disposition toward manipulation. Alyssa couldn't stand up without saying, "Do you want anything?" to all within a thirty-foot radius, though it was not charity that brought about this compulsion, nor duty—but a cold calculation that such acts of altruism add up to a karmic surplus, subconscious though this habit was.

That night, Alyssa was about to hop out for a midnight showing at Adult City, but first, Alyssa casually fit in an invitation of "Do you want anything?" for Ovid, who aloofly shook his chin; for Anna, who smilingly said, "no thank you"; and for Aaron, who caught Alyssa up in a long disquisition on his now-constant topic: how Ovid was "holding him back" from his goal of "actualization"—a word that Aaron got straight out of a book on pop psychology. (Aaron was sort of a pop psycho, and occasionally privy to cultish inclinations.)

Though Ovid ran roughshod on his plans that night, Aaron had to tough it out, if grudgingly. It was frustrating to him, this slow-moving childhood—inching along from birthday to birthday, so that Ovid was his official guardian, though Ovid was psychologically still a child. For Aaron saw him for what Ovid most obviously was: a virtuoso, and not an artist—an idiot savant minus a savant.

Anna was idly dishwashing, and Ovid, in a mood of comfort suiting a family man who always did his duty, slunk away to his study. As Ovid was thumbing lazily through an old translation of Thomas Mann's *Doctor Faustus*, thinking about which of his distractions would occupy him tomorrow, a loud discussion from his living room cut through his study's thin walls. Walking to his door and putting his cranium up against it, Ovid could distinguish a handful of particulars. Aaron was talking too loudly to Alyssa in his living room:

"What's up with Dad?" Aaron said, plopping down on a couch.

"I don't know, Aar." Alyssa put on a sour look. "Today I saw him picking through his trash for a lost manuscript. But Ovid has no manuscripts, lost *or* found."

"Why is Dad always wound up so tight? Is his imaginary book *that* important to anybody?" Aaron said, pausing, as was his habit, to try and think of a way to fit his inquiry into a film-quotation form. "It's his paranoia acting up again."

"But Ovid *has* a gift," Alyssa said. "Ovid is just too lazy to do anything with it."

"I know," said Aaron, "It's sad, actually. Ovid is good at all things, but with no passion for anything."

"Turning fifty must go down hard for him," said Alyssa, adding, "It's his last act."

Ovid put on a scowl. It was his forty-*ninth* birthday, and in no way was it his "last act," as Alyssa put it. (For Ovid's "last act," just skip to Book Six.)

"Yup," said Aaron. "Soon, his curtain will fall, and Ovid's ongoing drama—a 'Portrait of an Artist as a Young Madman'—must wrap up."

Naturally inclining towards gloom, Ovid saw, in this casual chat among his offspring, an admission that his work in this world would finally amount to nothing. His boss at OuLiPoCorp might call him out for his stupidity; Anna could dish out a crippling soliloquy on all of Ovid's flaws; visitors from Mars could launch an invasion tomorrow and body-snatch him, and spit him back out, proclaiming him worth not a mouthful; and *still*, Ovid's faith in his own artistic ambitions would stay.

But as soon as his own child could grasp that Ovid was just a middling sort—a Willy Loman of artists—Ovid thought that a word could sum up his biographical accumulations: *nothing*. An infinity could pass, and no mark of his would outlast him, no hook for his coat of immortal longing to hang upon—a coat with which a man might adorn his failings with comfort from a cold world.

And this flogging of Ovid did not stop with Aaron and Alyssa.

Still not an idol at fifty, Ovid's music would fall away, having not had any play on radio or TV. His visual art would not gain a following among a small group of hip, urban young folks who would savor a bond with him as an artist. A film fanatic, incurably so, Ovid still could not accomplish his plans to mix his passion for film with his fascination for political history, by filming an absurdist dramatization of Winston Churchill's biography.

Though his book got off to an auspicious start, and a handful of scholars would laud his first outing as an author, it quickly lost ground, and was torn apart by that industry's topmost critics, who took a shining to a similar book by a similar author, but an author who was from a working-class background, and his book had a similar nihilistic quality, but was a cocktail "mixt with two parts spunk, two parts sass and spit, and part pizzazz," as its blurb would happily inform us.

Cut apart by castrating critics, and fading slowly into obscurity, Ovid could only publish anonymously. Firmly midlist, his book would languish for months in a library stack, only to land in a discount bin at Dollar Barn. No local crowd would wait for him to sign autographs Sundays at Downtown Books.

Now, sitting by his ticking upright clock, a book lying flat on his lap, with his twins loudly parlaying in his parlor, Ovid could withstand anything but this notion—that an all-consuming *nothing* was awaiting him, which burnt all things to ash.

This *nothing* cast a pall on his world, a shadow, growing numb within him, killing his pain, but with it, too, his aspirations, his lust for glory. "If this should go on," Ovid thought, "I can only wish for an animal mortality. My psychic animus, my soul, all my physical parts, too, will fall away."

What was Ovid to do with all this angst? Indulging it would only fill its hungry mouth, and patronizing it could diminish him into a dark obscurity from which Ovid might not spring again.

Part Two

As a young man, Ovid was worldly and ambitious. Growing up in Britain, flying all around Asia in his youth—to India, Thailand, and Hong Kong—and abruptly moving to Boston to study at Harvard as a young child, was jarring. Finally graduating (at halfway to thirty, as old as his own son now was), Ovid was a young man, lacking in maturity, but full of can-do spirit. Ovid had a missionary's conviction that his calling was to do good in this world. To this day, Ovid is naturally both a scholar, and incurably romantic.

This background did allow Ovid to stick his foot into so many doors of so many corporations, including an illustrious publishing outfit, OuLiPoCorp. OuLiPoCorp had grown so big that it now had not only a books division, but a film studio, two TV stations, a radio station, a shopping mall, a toy factory, a hospital wing, an industrial manufacturing plant, a political lobbying association, a Third-World colony, and a black-ops organization with platoons as far away as Afghanistan,

Pakistan, Kazakhstan, Tajikistan, Kyrgyzstan, and all Stans. Ovid had no inkling of what OuLiPoCorp's grand mission was—or that OuLiPoCorp was actually a think-tank that had grown so big that it built its own think-army, and now was a rival not just to corporations, but nations, too.

In its vast, sprawling, clumsy lack of focus, OuLiPoCorp was a good match for Ovid's awkward fumbling toward glory through any kind of art. Though what was disappointing to Ovid, as a young man, was *which* door his foot got stuck in: that of OuLiPoCorp's accounting division. Ovid soon found that moving out of accounting and into divisions such as publishing or film or radio was a virtual impossibility. But a good salary, a good location, and an inclination toward comfort brought about Ovid's gradual submission to his lot.

His initial rank at OuLiPoCorp was that of an "Assistant Accountant's Accounting Assistant," though Ovid was not an accountant by training. Ovid had a skill for monotony—to truck through, day by day, in a world of doldrums, without complaint. His boss was constantly applauding his ability to sit still and go through a particularly humdrum day uncomplainingly. "That Ovid knows how to sit still!" his monthly job appraisal might say, or "Ovid Dullann can crunch data all day without falling unconscious!" If OuLiPoCorp would only host its own Olympics, giving out awards for a Just-Sitting-Around marathon or a Working-All-Day dash, Ovid would win so much gold that it would crush him.

All Ovid had to do was wait, and soon his status as "Assistant Accountant's Accounting Assistant" would turn into "Assistant Accountant's Assistant Accountant" (which may not sound as though it is any indication of upward mobility, but which, if you think about it, did switch his primary noun from "Assistant" to "Accountant").

This, in Ovid's world, was a significant triumph: His job was a titanic ship about to lift anchor and sail.

Ovid's only pal in Accounting was Durand Durand, a young guy with a lost-soul quality, just as socially awkward as Ovid, and just as gloomy. Durand Durand was a film fanatic, too, with a particular affinity for Cold War sci-fi. Ovid and Durand would talk for hours about Flash Gordon, arguing about which film incarnation did most harm to its comic strip's original vision.

Durand Durand's hair was always in disarray, but his work station was always tidy, giving off an air of a man with a paralyzing phobia of chaos—an OCD SOB—but also a man who forgot to look into his bathroom mirror of a morning.

Durand Durand was autistic, but his was a high-functioning autism. An illustration: At lunch, whilst staring straight at OuLiPoCorp building's south wall, Durand would count all its bricks—sitting on a picnic chair, nibbling banana and mango from his cold fruit cup with a plastic spoon. Durand Durand was always counting things, just as Dustin Hoffman would as Raymond Babbitt in *Rain Man*, though not so quickly, and usually off by a lot.

Contrary to Raymond Babbitt's autism, Durand Durand didn't mind folks touching him. In fact, his own habit of touching was obnoxious. Occasionally, Ovid thought that Durand Durand's diagnosis of autism was a half-truth: that Durand Durand was just about as autistic as Ovid was... but as for that, Ovid thought, "Am I autistic, too? Or am I just a hypochondriac?"

During his first month at OuLiPoCorp, Durand Durand had to justify, to an OuLiPoCorp consulting firm, his inability to act socially around ordinary non-accountants, so Durand Durand had to admit in public that his brain didn't work as a "normal" brain did. What Durand had *said* was that his diagnosis was a mild form of autism, but what all his OuLiPian cohorts *thought* was said was that Durand is an "Ass Burglar," and so Durand was stuck with that nominal insult: "Ass Burglar": OuLiPoCorp's unofficial mascot.

Ovid took pity on Durand Durand. As a childhood victim, in his own right, of a rough local rugby champ, Ovid thought that acts of bullying should not carry into adulthood, and his instinct was to stick up for Durand Durand. But no such opportunity was to occur. For as you know, that brand of bullying is straight-to-TV drama, and OuLiPoCorp's accounting division was, by contrast, as dull as a spot of black paint on a black canvas.

Ovid had to work all day in a gray, monotonous, soul-killing building—Sixth Floor, Room 636, a big, cubical auditorium full of dividing walls forming small cubical work units. His was an industrial building, all plastic, glass, and iron. Amidst a sylvan wood, this glass building stuck out ithy-phallically, as though stabbing its tip into a vast vaginal sky, trying to touch our sun with its iron sputum.

All in all, Ovid and OuLiPoCorp got along swimmingly. But on his down days, idly passing hour upon hour, shuffling and filing and computing, Ovid thought of running away.

Ovid was not without his days of dissipation. For a short month (you know which month I'm talking about—that particularly *short* month following January and prior to March), Ovid was put in a city jail for crashing his truck into a cop car. If it didn't occur in Wisconsin, Ovid's public intoxication and drunk driving would warrant a stint in prison. But Wisconsin's liquor lobby had cut away for so long at its drunk-driving laws that you couldn't punish a man too harshly for *anything* to do with alcohol.

A car-crash was as common a sight on its highways as a billboard.

As an accountant, and as a whitish-collar criminal, Ovid got out of prison whilst still awaiting trial, making bond, and thinking that prison was now a thing out of a distant past. But prison would stay in back of Ovid's mind as an historical low point in his adulthood—a dark past that would put a blight on all his days.

Look at Ovid's mug shot now: a gigantic cranium, ovoid, oblong, skin busy with pock-marks. Ovid's look is a cross of all kinds of looks, uncomfortably hybrid, as though a photo caught him in mid-morph: bushy brows with thin tails; dark pupils with bright umbra; giant flaring nostrils on a small, flat lump of skin; top lip broad, bottom lip narrow; dark brown hair with natural blond highlights—a light dusting of salt. His jowls sag down slightly, as wrinkly as a scrotum hanging from his chin.

Ovid's shadow casts an amorphous blob—globular, a snow-man walking in slow motion—and in fact Ovid will occasion-ally adorn his shirts with coal-black buttons and, in a particular mood, don a top-hat and cigar, just for show (an unusual flour-ish for a dullard such as Ovid Dullann). As if this wasn't a satisfactory justification for putting Ovid away in an asylum, Ovid always had his duds fit with a tag that said simply "Ovid," as though an imaginary burglar was planning to rob him of all his things, including his shirt, from his own back.

A bit of a skinflint, Ovid is thrifty to a fault. His motto is "If I don't got it, I don't want it." And this philosophy spans all sorts of things, from cars to clothing to food to prophylactics. But it was not always thus.

Third Part

Ovid first ran into Anna at a party in Boston, during a six-month span in which Ovid was a Harvard grad, but hadn't found his first job at OuLiPoCorp's Madison branch. Raymond Q, an OuLiPoan (and, in about a month or two, Ovid's boss), was hosting a shindig in honor of Harry Math, a mutual pal of Ovid and Anna's, who had a baby coming in two months.

Ovid, Raymond, and Harry had an odd dynamic: shy individually, but as a trio, full of braggadocio. Apart, Raymond and Harry had almost no social skills (nor did Ovid, obviously). But as a group, it was almost as though a garrulous imp was inhabiting Ovid and his marching band of charming oxymorons.

That day, Harry was also toasting his first job opportunity. Failing to find a job at OuLiPoCorp, Harry was about to start out as an instructor at Madison Public High School. (Soon, Harry and Ovid would go through a vicious falling-out, as Raymond Q would pass up on hiring Harry in favor of Ovid.)

Harry had always had a crush on Anna, and from that day forward, Harry thought of Ovid as his rival. But it was Polly—a girl whom Harry was dating, and whom Harry was now about to marry—Polly, who was carrying his child, for whom this baby-party was now plugging along.

On such occasions, it is typical for visitors to abstain from drink, in sympathy for this baby-carrying woman who cannot sip a drip of alcohol. Polly Math, in particular, was frail and moody, with a naturally anxious disposition, a girl of whom you would not want to run afoul.

Practically a baby in his own right, Ovid was still too young to drink anyway. Without social lubrication, this "party" was a sad affair, passing slowly, hour by hour, but it was just as Ovid was about to slip out during a round of Baby Bingo that Anna would walk in.

Harry and Polly Math's dining-room was a bright, colorful array of upright things. It was spic-and-span, down to its surprisingly un-dusty China hutch, brimming with display-only sugar bowls and napkin rings. Anna, by way of contrast, was falling-down drunk. From across this living-room span, Ovid found this sight thrilling. Ovid had always had a morbid fascination with girls on a downward spiral, and at first blush, Anna's situation brought him joy of this dark kind.

But Ovid was quickly drawn toward Anna as a woman, not just as an illustration of man's capacity for his own ruin.

What was Ovid to do with this attraction? Ovid was not a frat boy, and Anna was not an anonymous sorority girl; random and casual couplings did not suit him. Ovid thought, "If a man hits on a drunk woman, it is immoral. But!… If a drunk man hits on a drunk woman, it is all fair." So Ovid did what any logician would do in a similar quandary: drink until his own inhibition was drowning.

In a hazy glow of liquid light, Anna and Ovid did what wayward youths do, blazing with hormonal glory: carry on a short flirtation, drink until hazy, and quickly hook up at a party. It is only with morning's arrival that Ovid saw what a "catch" Anna actually was. Though Ovid had long found comfort in knowing that many fish swam in his social pond, in Anna, Ovid had found his ovum, and was now not happy dining on anything but caviar.

So Ovid did what Ovid understood: how to charm a girl through a curtain of linguistic fog. A flurry of words, with an occasional lucid point or two, but mostly bloviating, was his usual approach to courtship. This cloud of confusion, so Ovid thought, brought upon a slight paralysis—just that right amount, for his victim to start thinking, "OK, I put up with this guy for this long, and I'm still around. Why? Am I actually drawn to his company? What am I doing with this guy? Is it an attraction just waiting to hit?"

As a young man, Ovid was an avid aficionado of coins—a numismatist—and all Ovid could talk about was his mint-condition Franklin half-dollars. Moving from this topic to his *Star Wars* infatuation, and—finally—to his darling idol, Winston Churchill, Ovid did not allow any room for his companion to slip a word in, straight *or* diagonally.

Luckily for Ovid, Anna was looking for a savior, and this boring but mildly ambitious young man fit this mold. His odd mix of gloomy dissipation and sunny stoicism was a paradox that Anna was curious to unfold. (Anna was that sort of woman who unfolds origami animals, too.)

An odd courtship was about to start—a courtship consisting mostly of talk. Anna didn't go to Harvard, as Ovid had, but Anna was a quick study. If anything, Ovid had to catch up with Anna's vocabulary, which was full of urban lingo and gang slang from Anna's "lost days" as a runaway, panhandling in Toronto's slums. (It was out of such a past, too, that Anna got so many tattoos, including a "tramp stamp" that was actually a gang's way of branding its "mamas.")

Knowing that it is traditional to buy a woman a bunch of lilacs or carnations, Ovid found a local florist but, as it was now autumn, Ovid could find only mums. As Anna was living in a two-room flat, and not in a building of Anna's own, Ovid had to plant mums all around his own patio (long prior to its burning down at Aaron's hands). Looking back on it now, Ovid might think that a solitary man planting mums in dry soil is a fitting symbol for what was soon on its way.

Anna thought Ovid was gay at first, which conclusion Anna had drawn by adding up so many minor signals—his constant Bambi-blinking, his slight lisp, his roundabout way of talking, planting mums around his patio—but soon found out that it was not so. Anna also found that asking if Ovid was gay brought about this humorous dissimulation: "Oh… huh, I think… that's not… what I'm trying to say is… I couldn't… do you… what do you think?"

Anna was a young woman of surprising good looks: short black hair falling all around in a sloppy but alluring array; twin kohl-black orbs almost too big for such a flimsy scaffolding (a comically small nasal protrusion), as though popping out of its cavity. A tiny mouth, as if unfit to swallow solid food, but only to drink it in liquid form, through a straw. Anna shows a slim chin, a wan color, and a hangdog look with a surprising capacity to charm, bringing about (as it invariably will) a man's savior instinct.

But this gothic portrait of Anna is cut short by this insight: that Anna is ticklish. With Anna, a dour mood can turn to instant sanguinity with a giggling fit. You wouldn't think such girlish mirth was a possibility coming from this brooding blossom, but a burst of hilarity from Anna during a slaphappy fit would handily undo this assumption.

Although Anna, as anybody who knows Anna will say, has a right to brood. Anna had it bad growing up—as an orphan in an institution, with no mom or dad or guardian. Graduating high school was cold consolation, as Anna had no job and no backup plan. As a young adult, too, Anna was stuck in a rut, turning into a bad habit of hard-drinking, turning into hard-vomiting, falling unconscious, waking up and going back to drinking right away.

It was into this sordid history that Anna and Ovid would cross paths. It was a whirlwind courtship, and within a month, Ovid and Anna would stand at an altar, forming a nuptial bond.

It took many months to kill off Anna's habit: months of going back and forth to Alcoholics Anonymous (which a local patron saw fit to host in a room with no windows in a drab community building), only to find that Anna had snuck in a flask of bourbon; losing Anna for days, and picking Anna up (actually having to *pick Anna up*) at a local bar; trying to bring Anna back to Alcoholics Anonymous, just to watch Anna jump out of a moving car, for which folly Anna paid with two ugly scars running up and down both arms; taking Anna to Saint Mary's Hospital, sitting by Anna's cot in a crowd of sick, poor folk (and poor Ovid with his mysophobia!).

It's hard to say how Anna could transition, from such a long habit of dissipation and non-conformism in youth, to turn into, as an adult, what amounts to Ovid's lapdog. But Ovid had that capacity of stirring within a woman—and Anna in particular—a dormant nurturing instinct.

This is as good a clarification of that history as any: that Ovid had stood so tall, for so long, as a virtuous paragon—and Anna had sunk so low as this duo's wayward half, a pariah—that it took an act of God to stir up this comforting dichotomy. But an act of God *did* occur. Upon miscarrying, Anna took a vow to quit alcohol for good.

And now that dynamic was starting to unfold: Anna was proving worthy of a family, and Ovid was looking for a way

25

out—for any opportunity to show that it was not silicon pumping through him, but blood—warm and crimson and voluminous.

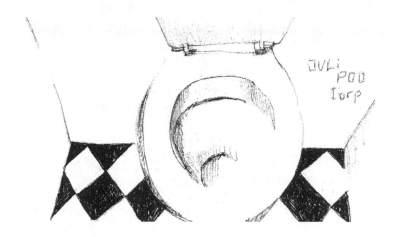

Part Four

At almost fifty, it was Ovid's turn to numb his mind with drink.

Ovid soon found that vomiting in a public lavatory did not satisfy his thirst, but only dug him low into his abyss. His mind still functioning at capacity, it would go on mocking his body's fragility, as if in total dissociation from it.

Ovid took up churchgoing, too, and stood in a back row during mass on Sunday. This laity, full of Baptists, could, without thinking about it, throw its arms up into vacant air, swaying to a rhythm of Psalms. As this song was finishing, Ovid thrust his arms up, too, just to try it out, and caught a quick look at his own dark form in a fading brass door, as if in a dull mirror. With bright rays from a hanging light outlining his arms, it did look as though Ovid, holding his hands up high and straight, was actually a man at gunpoint.

As Ovid would finish his obligatory Sunday visit to church, it was not with church organs sounding in his brain, but with a trailing sound of a churchgoing goody-goody coughing loudly during a musical hiatus.

In a sorrowful mood, Ovid would turn to old comforts: a marathon of Cold War sci-fi films, starting with *Flight to Mars*, in which a dying Martian civilization is too proud to admit it is falling apart, so it imprisons a visiting human astronaut and his companions, hoping to occupy his land of origin. By its tragic conclusion, Ovid was bawling, still a bit tipsy from his orgy of liquor.

Upon finishing his Cold War sci-fi marathon, Ovid found an odd thing going on. His bottom was stuck to his couch cushion, and his will to stand up was draining away. His pupils in full dilation, jaw slacking, a strand of drool running down from his chin, Ovid was turning into an audiovisual-consumption apparatus, a tool for watching: a sci-fi robot in his own right.

Cold War sci-fi would soon transition into horror camp, and horror camp would turn into buddy action films, and buddy action films would pass on in favor of bio-pics. And just as Ovid thought that his TV addiction had found its nadir, bio-pics lost out to sit-coms and rom-coms and dot-coms (programs consisting only of popular viral films: cats playing piano, acrobats running and jumping around in an urban playground, clumsy idiots falling down a flight of stairs whilst a humiliating soundtrack plays on a constant loop).

Worst of all was *Your Show!*—a program that sought to portray what "actual folks" do all day—by putting a "common man" in a room and simply filming him in all his habits and flaws. But *Your Show!* had ridiculous assumptions about its public, which was primarily poor or working class, but not half as crass or barbarous as its originators thought. If ratings shot down a point or two, *Your Show!* would bring in a martial arts "fighting champion" to pick a fight with him, or throw in a psychologically dubious blond succubus to draw him in, to play with his mind in daily dramatizations of what "You"—a common man—might go through in your "common" sort of world.

For a full thirty days, Ovid was stuck to his couch, abandoning it only for occasional visits to his bathroom and to go to work at OuLiPoCorp. But at OuLiPoCorp, too, Ovid would sit down in his chair, staring into his lap, as though still watching TV, awaiting any sort of vivid psychological stimulus.

During his days at OuLiPoCorp, Ovid also found odd things. Whilst filing contracts, Ovid found, in back of a filing tray, a can of manila-color paint and thought, "Why would anybody in this gray building think of using a can of manila-color paint?" Upon this thought, it hit Ovid that OuLiPoCorp was going back and changing history, using manila paint to blot out words on its official manuals, affidavits, authorization forms—anything in print, and not in digital format. In fact, much of his old work—now that Ovid was so suspicious as to go back and look at it—had a splotch of paint, or a torn-out paragraph, as though hiding an important word or fact.

Last, and most important of all, Ovid thought how odd it was that OuLiPoCorp was installing a local circuit cam in his work unit, monitoring his work habits.

This brought Ovid to think that his own world was turning into a kind of *Your Show!*, in which an anonymous TV community was spying on his actions without his knowing it. But Ovid was *not* a common man; Ovid was an uncommon animal—a giant panda or sloth—a sasquatch, possibly, or dodo bird—hardly an animal at all.

Ovid put his paranoid thoughts into a "box" and put that box into an "attic" of his mind, and shut that attic with a "lock," just as his prim British nanny had taught him as a boy.

So now, avoiding his own work, and moving out into OuLiPoCorp building's common room, Ovid would mill around that vast grassland in which you could always find OuLiPoCorp's junior staff grazing. Running into Durand Durand, Ovid struck up a dialog. Chatting up Durand Durand, his only work buddy, Ovid found out that this oddball was not just autistic, but insomniac, staying up past midnight, waking up at 4 a.m., a film addict stuck in front of a glowing box, as Ovid was. And though Durand Durand had no family, his comic-book-and-toy "family" was just as gratifying to him as an actual family.

Ovid and Durand Durand, as it would turn out, had much in common. (But, as both Ovid and Durand Durand fit into that group of "uncommon" sorts, this still did not qualify Ovid as a "common man," for whom a *Your Show!* situation was a possibility.)

"I cannot dismiss this thought," Ovid said to Durand Durand, "that OuLiPoCorp is watching us."

"Right now, in this instant?" Durand Durand sought to clarify.

"Always," Ovid said.

"Hmmm…," said Durand Durand. "I don't doubt it. Statistically, it is a high probability that, on any particular day, any individual is caught on film for four-to-six hours."

"But by whom?" Ovid said.

"All I know is that statistic," said Durand Durand. "Sorry. I can't run a synoptic analysis on it."

"That's OK, but I am finding it hard to function, just thinking about an anonymous man or woman watching us." Ovid couldn't stop looking around, for signs of anybody looming with a digital gizmo, filming this production.

"It is a low probability that a man or woman is watching continuously. And if so, it is poor organizational policy, as it would distract paid labor from analytical work. A basic AI program could probably do basic facial cognition tasks."

An AI program! Ovid thought. *Is that who is watching us?* Ovid said, "All I know is that I am lost, and it is a comfort to know a man such as you, Durand, who won't contradict my paranoia, but in fact confirms it."

"Lost?" Durand said. "But this is OuLiPoCorp Building C. Your workroom is practically in front of us: Just go straight and turn right," indicating that tiny room into which Ovid pours all his days (not including Saturdays and Sundays).

"I don't know. Am I afraid that OuLiPoCorp is watching? Or am I afraid that *nobody* is watching?"

"If it isn't OuLiPoCorp, who is it?" Durand Durand said.

"An AI program? A four-dollar-an-hour working stiff? A vast right-wing conspiracy?"… "God?" Ovid almost said, but cut it short. Of all things that Ovid and Durand Durand had in common, most significantly, both had doubts about God.

Fifth Part

On a Thursday in autumn, walking on an asphalt path of that Wisconsin town in which our protagonist was whiling away his adulthood, Ovid found a kiosk and, among ads for dog-walking jobs and calls for bass guitarists, saw a billboard broadcasting all kind of distractions for stray pupils from UW-Madison, or anybody looking to turn his world into a grand playground. Snow sports, such as skiing and snowboarding; boat trips, including rafting, tubing, kayaking, and so forth; bicycling; Outward Bound; parachuting, hang-gliding, hot air ballooning... and skydiving.

Notwithstanding his own profound abyss, Ovid had not lost his inborn curiosity. How was Ovid to lift his mind out of this rut? Inspiration struck. This is what Ovid was waiting for. "I'm going skydiving," Ovid said to his family that day. "I am finally grasping what I ought to do in this world."

"Wait. What's going on?" said Anna, who by now was Ovid's practical half.

"Don't you know? This world is not a prank, nor any part of it a sham! Walt Whitman said that. I don't want to throw away my days laboring for nothing—painting so-so art, writing books with no plots, making music with no rhythm."

"So... what is it you want?" Anna could look scarily anxious at such an instant.

"I want a dynamic soul, and I want to run away and fill my biography," Ovid said, as convincingly as Ovid could.

"That's a cop-out. I don't know what to think.... Is this about you turning fifty?"

"That is not it at all," said Ovid. "That is not what I'm saying at all."

"So why talk about it? Why not just go off, as old dogs do?" Anna was chopping onions, and Ovid thought that *that* was why Anna was crying. "What do you want? Absolution? My approval?"

"I'm not trying to justify it, and I'm not making an apology. I told you out of obligation. Now I'm going." And with that, Ovid was out of his front door.

Ovid took along Durand Durand, his only pal from work, a compatriot in OuLiPoCorp's Lost World—a world consisting of filing accounts, doing payroll, crunching data, in addition to his main task, which was assistant-accounting.

Ovid thought that Durand Durand, a young man with sky-diving know-how, could assist him if things got out of control. Durand Durand brought along his Palm Pilot (this was 2004), and was composing lyrical ballads on it (a form that is popular owing to a handful of British Romantics, including William Wordsworth), for Gina, an Asian manicurist whom Durand Durand had run into at a local shopping mall and was totally gaga for (but who was obviously not as fond of Durand Durand, as Gina didn't tag along that day, or any day).

Ovid was playing rap music loudly from his car, as if it could stall his graying hair and aging skin. This morning, only an hour away from a launching pad for his first skydiving trip,

Ovid was anxious, but was starting to succumb to anticipation, turning to thrill, changing into abandon, and finally subsiding into a willful tranquility, as a moth out of his chrysalis attains maturity in an instant.

"What'cha workin' on?" Ovid said. His car spat out clouds of dirty smog, and bugs would splat on his front window.

"A lipogram," Durand said. "Why?"

"I don't know; I'm curious. I'm an author, too. Though I hardly finish anything. I had a book out long ago: *Marginalia*. Do you know it?"

Durand Durand said nothing.

"So what's a lipogram?" Ovid said quickly, just to fill a void.

"You limit your words by omitting particular symbols, such as a A, B, C, or D, from a work—but I do all kinds of constraint writing: a story of all nouns ("Buzz Aldrin, astronaut. Moon-walk. Trip, back. Oops. Mars."), or a haiku with just six words ("Unassumingly / phantasmagoria lit / upon our lampposts"). Or a pantoum with a million words, if you want, as long as it is a valid constraint," said Durand, touching his Palm Pilot constantly.

Ovid didn't know what a pantoum was (it's a Malaysian form in which you copy your first and third row from your first stanza into rows two and four in stanza two, and so on), but didn't think much of it. "Son of a bitch. That sounds tough."

"It is, but it's not so hard that you couldn't try it, *just for fun*." Durand Durand could hardly look up from his gizmo for a word or two.

Ovid's gloom almost took him again. His last writing plan "just for fun" was back in 2002—a story about a girl with a masochistic fantasy of wax dripping on various body parts, in a compromising position, as a man with an unusual surgical situation was stimulating his own artificial organ. "This is disgusting," Ovid said four days following his writing of it, and could not finish it.

"So, this 'lipogram' stuff, did it start with OuLiPoCorp?" Ovid said.

"Yup," was Durand Durand's bland, monosyllabic communication.

"A-ha! I thought so. So, it's manufacturing, basically, and not writing at all," was Ovid's claim.

"You say it's not 'writing,' but, as I am *writing* it, I know that it is; so I think that what you actually want to say is that it's not 'raw'—it's not Chuck Palahniuk or Chuck Bukowski," Durand Durand said, looking mad with passion (oddly, for an autistic agnostic insomniac such as Durand). "I don't swallow my food raw, so why should I do so with writing?"

"OK, OK," said Ovid, to shut him up, saying, "So... you don't go for sushi." This oddball pair spun through rural Wisconsin roads until arriving at launch point.

Durand Durand and Ovid's airlift was a dull gray color, but with a luminous, bluish tint showing through. Ducts and tubing lay out on its floor, and a book of highly difficult-to-follow instructions for an array of buttons and controls sat on a stand, abutting a pilot's chair, with a tag that said, in sloppy handwriting, *Titanium Falcon*. It was, in fact, a sight right out of *Star Wars*, both futuristic and old, as if coming from long, long ago in a galaxy far, far away. Would a young Harrison Ford, as Han Solo, pull in for an impromptu dialog with Obi-Wan? It was all so phony, Ovid almost thought it wouldn't fly. This aviator, though, was a pro, and in fact a bit smug, as Han Solo was.

Han Solo's ship took off, taking Ovid and Durand Durand with it. Ovid was sitting on its floor, and so was Durand, and a group of six young guys from UW-Madison, out for a thrill. Ovid was an old man in this crowd—practically Yoda by comparison.

Aloft at this point, all talk among this company was unstrung. Admitting frailty was such a failing within this group that, upon *Titanium Falcon*, Ovid was losing his cool, but had to act happy about it anyway. Ovid had a compulsion to sprawl out on its floor—to go horizontal—which was hard to fight off.

"No doubts about doing this?" Durand Durand said, intuiting his companion's discomfort (which autistics don't usually do).

"Not at all," said Ovid. "Why?"

"I don't know," Durand Durand said, "Skydiving is basically dropping from a six-thousand-foot summit to solid ground with nothing to stop you but a canvas mat."

But prior to Ovid saying anything, a guy with a Mohawk hairdo cut in.

"You call this a 'canvas mat'?" Mohawk guy said, brandishing his backpack. "It's not just a tarp in a bag, man; this is our most vital tool, and don't jinx us by talking that way. It's bad luck."

To which Durand Durand said, "Call it what you will—luck or skill or 'God's will'—nothing you say can avoid this fact: In half an hour, you will jump out of a moving aircraft, and if that bag malfunctions, so will you."

"I call it luck," said Mohawk guy, to his buddy.

"No such thing as luck," Ovid said automatically, as if quoting a film. Adding, as if to distract Durand Durand, "So what about this lipogram?"

"What about it?"

"Why don't you say it aloud, if you know it?"

"Right now? As a monolog?" said Durand.

"Why? Is it a dialog?"

"No, but... OK." Durand Durand got into a position, and his physiognomy took on a dolorous cast.

Humans (A Lyrical Ballad in Six Stanzas)

for Gina

First stanza, a lipogram on H:

A fox has flown into a cupid's coat—

bird-wings of Icarus, *Built in Taiwan*

on folds of plastic, faint, and faintly worn

(And amply vast for two of us to try on).

Stanza two, a lipogram on U:

And driving arrows into immortal hands—

a stigmata for how far a man may fall—

so that this girl from China or Japan

thinks of this man (who knows no passion at all).

Third stanza, a lipogram on M:

But I could woo you with six radiant stanzas

to yolk us with, within, without, to wit:

Although I hail originally from Kansas,

I know that this girl, Gina, and I fit.

Stanza four, a lipogram on A:

No profound unity is forming on a

tip of orchid pistil, or drop of snow;

38

It is within us only, such joining

(two souls with but a spirit singly flow).

Fifth stanza, a lipogram on N:

I applaud this totality of ours,

But it is partly horror, too, I savor—

A moral fall, short of purity,

For us to so voluptuously flavor.

Stanza six, a lipogram on S:

Now I will go and quit our world for good,

Not wait around for ambiguity

To undo all that my conviction could.

I will to you my land, and an annuity.

"What do you think?" said Durand Durand.

"Hmmmm… It's awkward," said Ovid. "I'll chalk it up to this: A romantic lyric is its own constraint."

"Awkward? How so?" said Durand Durand.

"Two things: First of all, why don't you know if Gina is from China or Japan?"

"Gina's folks got Gina from AAA (Asian-baby Adoption Association), and didn't try too hard to find out about what country Gina was from. Anyway, it is only our souls that count, right? Not this body, not our skin color," said Durand Durand.

Pointing at his companion, Ovid said, "This guy is such a romantic." To Durand Durand, Ovid said, "I don't know. It counts for a lot if Gina is from Tokyo, or Shanghai; if Gina was born in Osaka, or Saigon, of Bangkok. It also counts for a lot if Durand Durand is from Kansas or not. Is it that you hail from Kansas, as you say, or that you couldn't find anything good to fit with 'stanzas'? Anyway, it also sounds gloomy and suicidal. You talk about 'your will,' and thoughts of 'quitting this world,' and all that. It's too sad-clown and sorrowful, and too blatant about it."

Durand Durand was looking blatantly sad-clown and sorrowful. "What should I do with it?" Durand Durand said.

"Scrap it, and start again. That's what I'd do," Ovid said.

"But you don't finish anything," said Durand Durand, "as you just said."

"But I'm always starting things! I'm just saying, it's lacking; in what way, I cannot say, but it's lacking."

Durand Durand was taciturn now, almost sour. "I just want to point out that 'Ovid Dullann' has a fitting anagram." Durand said.

"Hah! Anagrams now, is it? What is with you and gimmicks?" Ovid was sorry now that Durand Durand was along for his first skydiving trip. All Durand Durand could talk about was his suicidal fantasy, and Ovid was just now moving away from all that.

"You should try it," Durand Durand said, finally.

"Try what?" Ovid said, thinking about Durand Durand's suicidal fantasy.

"Anagrams, lipograms, lyrical ballads. You should try all forms of writing, until you got nothing good to try."

"Lot of good it's doing for you," said Ovid tartly. "Lipograms? I'd try liposuction first!"

"OK, boys," said Martin Crunch, captain of this skydiving group, standing up abruptly. "Grab your buddy and stand at jump point."

Looking at Durand Durand and Ovid, Martin Crunch said, "Which of you is top, and which is bottom?"

"Hmmm," said Ovid, "I am a top, wouldn't you say, Durand?"

"Actually," said Durand Durand, "top, in this situation, only assigns which of us has most skydiving know-how."

"But I am just not a bottom," said Ovid.

"OK," said Durand Durand, taking Ovid's hand and bringing him to jump-point, buckling in, and jumping out first, with Ovid following on his back.

"Whooooo-hooooo!" Ovid's shout rang out through gray sky.

"Look down," Durand Durand said, and Ovid did, and spiraling towards a flat horizon, Ovid saw what you could only call "nirvana" (sans Kurt Cobain and David Grohl). For Ovid, it was paralyzing. But for Durand Durand, it was an opportunity.

"I'm going," said Durand Durand, unlatching his strap, and falling away. As his body spun off, Durand Durand had drawn Ovid's cord out so that Ovid would stay afloat, parachuting slowly down, as Durand Durand's body spilt into vacant sky. Ovid had to watch as his companion shrunk into a dot, and into oblivion.

His own way down was slow, arduous, and painstaking, tugging on strings to pull him this way and that. And Ovid's horror, upon watching his companion finish his fall with a splat, as calm and casual as a bug on a window, was gravity-inducing. Ovid got caught in a rampant wind and, lacking Durand Durand's skill at skydiving, was now flying toward a suburban district.

Ovid simply could not wrap his mind around it. Was Ovid still in his living room, watching TV, or having a hallucination? Was humanity truly just a waiting room, and was humankind simply idling his days until an individual saw fit to opt out, totally at random, jumping out of a blank sky and falling to his doom, in a grand suicidal splash?

This gloomy mood, in Ovid, took a turn inward, and it was his own mortality now that Ovid saw on a flat, growing horizon.

Stuck in a philosophical loop, Ovid thought, "In trying to distract my mind from its gloom, I was only avoiding this hard truth: This world has no kingdom of bliss, no paradisiacal city in its clouds. Humankind can glorify only what is unknown to him, and, as physics imparts to us what was in past days mystical, dying is his only way of joining with what is truly unknown."

From his vista in a vacant sky, Ovid saw clouds dissipating, birds swirling, and solid ground, with its plant and animal population, approaching him.

Falling, Ovid thought, "I am past all youthful fantasy now, all hoping for a functional world, all utopias, and I can but carry this cynical wisdom to my doom."

Ovid thought about what Alyssa would say: "Dad, you think too much." But it was Durand Durand, his romantic autistic insomniac pal, with whom Ovid was only passingly familiar, who had an ability to fathom him that Alyssa did not.

As his balloon of canvas got caught in a gust of wind, Ovid was blown into a backyard pool, in which a family of four (a man, a woman, a girl, and a boy, just as Ovid's family was) was obliviously swimming. Looking up at him, this man, a family patriarch, was startlingly similar to Ovid. And this woman, who was clutching his arm, was also startlingly similar to Anna. This boy and girl, too, simulacra of Aaron and Alyssa.

But this family, for all its similarity, just saw a man fall from a gray sky into its back yard—a thing that just did not occur in Ovid's family. Soon his right arm was rising out of this pool, as a man took Ovid up and onto his back, and brought him a chair.

"You OK, buddy?" said this man, with a furrowing brow and jutting chin. "Durand Durand!" Ovid said, lazily lolling his skull around on its spinal column, "Durand Durand is cast out among our cosmos now."

"You did all that you could," said this man, knowing right away what Ovid was trying to say, and on this assumption, assuaging his guilt. "It's not your fault. Nothing could stop him from falling."

Though Ovid was mourning his buddy, Ovid's mind was still lost in TV-land, cycling through his catalog of quotations. As a film buff, Ovid couldn't stop thinking about that obnoxious Gus Van Sant film with Matt Damon and Robin Williams, particularly of a part in which a psychologist with a tragic history forms a bond with an iconoclastic prodigy (a janitor at MIT) and, in a moving climax, says to him, "It's not your fault…. It's not your fault…. It's not your fault….," trying to crack through his tough, Irish-Catholic, South-Boston armor by calling up his own history as a child who was hurt by his dad.

Not that it should imply anything about Ovid's childhood, which was cushy and soft by comparison.

Part Six

Ovid and this man, Konstantinos Diamantaras, had built up a rapport as two dads adrift in a confusing world, and not long into this companionship, Ovid was sitting in Konstantinos' dining room, having lunch with his family. Immigrants from Olympic country, Konstantinos and his family had Apollonian blood and Dionysian spirits. (Ovid's own blood was firmly Anglo-Saxon with a slight Gallic dilution.)

"Shouldn't you contact a constabulary?" said Mrs. Diamantaras, in an idiom typical of immigrants from Classical civilizations.

"Ovid is still in shock, Anzora," said Konstantinos, "from losing his pal, Durand Durand. You can wait until Ovid has his lunch, anyway. Authority is such poor company."

To Ovid, Konstantinos said, "Tonight, Mrs. Diamantaras and I will host a party. You will go, too?"

"I would if I could, but I can't so I won't," said Ovid, quoting again. "My family is waiting."

"Bring your kids. Bring Anna. It will all work out OK." Konstantinos had a knack for inspiring faith in his plans. It was this quality, Ovid thought, that could allow such a man as Konstantinos to own his own McMansion with its own swimming pool.

"OK," said Ovid, "I will try." Having lost a companion to a skydiving mishap, Ovid was now gaining a companion, too.

That night, Ovid brought his family to Diamantaras' party: an occasion for introducing his family. "This is Anna, and Aaron, and Alyssa," said Ovid, displaying his brood with a slight bow and a brush of his arm. "My family."

All in all, Ovid's family and Konstantinos' family got along swimmingly: kids mingling with adults, and guys with girls, without discrimination. Food was abundant, starting with a salad bar that had a full stock of spinach, tomato, onion, broccoli, bacon bits, croutons, tofu, hummus, baba ganoush—any toppings that fit in with this motif. As a main dish, for carnivorous company, a rack of lamb; for omnivorous visitors, Atlantic shrimp in risotto; and for his host, who took no fish, fowl, or poultry, an avocado sandwich with mustard and Havarti with dill. Ovid was practically drooling onto his shirt.

With a trio playing (a pianist showing off his organ, a flautist flouting his fluting skills, and a violinist strumming his strings with a bow), this background band ran from strings to winds to drums (if you count a piano as a kind of drum); it was only missing horns and woodwinds. But this array of musical options would allow a gamut of sorts: classical, jazz, rock and roll, country, and, in a pitiful bid for mass popularity, pop music.

Aaron in particular was mingling with his hosts in a socially promiscuous way. It was unusual for him to draw a crowd, but such was his situation now. An aspiring Harry Houdini, Aaron was practicing magic, and on this occasion, doing a classic trick with a bunny and a hat. But a magic trick is not just a comforting illusion—it is also a way of using human gullibility to part a fool from his gold. And in fact, Aaron did try to con a tip or two out of this crowd.

To his dismay, Ovid found out that Konstantinos was also an OuLiPoan, as Ovid was—not a lowly assistant accountant, but a company bigwig. An itch of paranoia snuck up on him, snaking up his spinal cord and tickling his hind-brain. Upon finding out his story, though, Ovid saw Konstantinos as a man who got by through pulling up on his own bootstraps, not riding on coattails. Konstantinos was a living incarnation of Ovid's right brain, and Durand Durand was his antonym.

Through his hard work and chutzpah, Konstantinos was now managing OuLiPoCorp's Madison branch, bound only to his boss, Li Po—this company's originator. "So who *is* Li Po, and what is Mr. Po up to with all this OuLiPoCorp stuff?" Ovid thought of asking him, but had to clamp his lips shut to avoid sounding paranoid.

Konstantinos was trying to coax Ovid and his family to stay that night, and at sunup go on a fishing trip to Bass Park, and back for brunch. Though Ovid was too blind to pick up on it, Konstantinos was also ogling Anna.

"What's for brunch?"

"Oh, ordinary stuff: a croissant sandwich with Nova Scotia lox (just cold salmon, basically). Cappuccino. Banana yogurt for my son Frank." Konstantinos said. "Muffins."

Muffins! Ovid was longing for a muffin, particularly a cinnamon-raisin or spicy pumpkin, but torn in two by this quandary: to munch, or to mourn?

"I don't think so. I just lost a good pal," Ovid said, fogging up slightly. "Durand Durand was a son of a rabbi, so his family will sit shiva for him tomorrow. It would not look good to miss it on account of brunch, as much as I might want your cappuccino and muffins."

"OK. But you might want to go anyway, just for fun," said Konstantinos. "*Mi casa, su casa.*"

"Just for fun!" Ovid thought. "Ha!"

It was at Konstantinos' party that Ovid would cross paths again with Raymond Q, now an art aficionado who had his own studio in Chicago, only two hours or so away from Madison. Raymond sold prints and paintings in his showroom, but not too long ago took up publishing in small print runs for monographs or chapbooks that stood out as of particularly high quality.

Ovid was thinking about Durand Durand's last words (apart from "Look down" and "I'm going"). Ovid was curious about this "trying all forms of writing" to which Durand Durand was alluding, and curious about what an art critic thought of it.

"What do you think about lipograms?" Ovid said to Raymond Q.

"Urban philistinism," said Raymond, dismissing it all.

"I'm sorry, what is urban philistinism?" Ovid said.

"Four kinds of philistinism surround us: With rural philistinism, all art must contain a moral. No art form of any kind can contain ambiguity. It's all 'good guys' and 'bad guys,' usually concluding with a gunfight to show us how *our guys* always win. In suburban philistinism, you might think art is 'worthy of adoration,' or 'important to a thriving civilization,' but not as important as your job and your kids and your bills. It is, in sum, only a commodity in a world full of commodity.

"With urban philistinism, art is so out of touch with any-thing human that it is innovation without charm or joy. Art is just a symbol of sophistication, a parlor trick that witty artists play, which turns art into a highbrow sport of ironic pun-upsmanship."

Folding his arms and nodding throughout all of this, Ovid finally said, "So, which is most valid, as a valuation of art?"

Q said, "Of all philistinisms, I favor urban philistinism, on account of my living in a city. Andy Warhol was of this sort. And so was Jackson Pollack, you could say. If saying so wasn't such a philistinism in its own right, I would also put Pablo Picasso in this group."

"Wait... you said *four* philistinisms. What about this fourth philistinism? So far, I only know of rural, suburban, and urban," said Ovid.

"That kind of philistinism is so low that it is unworthy of discussion. This kind of philistinism is nihilism, apathy, a lack of any artistic outlook at all. This is Bart Simpson's phi-listinism, and Chairman Mao's philistinism (corporatism and communism both contain this common fault)."

Ovid could not stop thinking about this until dawn.

That day, Ovid did not go to Konstantinos' brunch, and did not sit shiva for his pal Durand Durand. Ovid was struck with a thirst so strong that nothing short of total satisfaction would do—to uphold Durand Durand's lipogrammatic spirit, starting out slowly, by writing a story omitting all words that contain an "A." Ovid took this thirst and spun it into a vow—that Ovid would not stop writing until Durand Durand's lipogram was born through him.

At first, Ovid *was* having fun, to a point that his industry did not strain at all. But soon Ovid was caught in a labyrinth of his own construction. Particularly, Ovid was stuck in a swamp of linguistic trash. How much cussing and gratuitous nudity could a man fit into a story?

Ovid's work was full of smut: A man who was born Dirty Dick (his own mom would call him Dirty Dick) is a working magician, or "illusionist," who puts on shows at a camp for kids who want to study "occultism," and who want to grow into wizards and warlocks (Ovid took pains to distinguish Wicca, which isn't actually magic but a spiritual philosophy, from Dirty Dick's kind of tricks). Many accusations against Dirty Dick, involving his magic wand, or "glow stick," show up to haunt his School of Hocus Pocus (which critics of his would call Dirty Dick's School of Hokum-Pokum).

On occasion, throughout this story's dialog, Ovid had his protagonist cry out such filthy things as, "I'm a dirty, shit-wiping, slit-sticking villain!" as Dirty Dick was attaining orgasm, sodomizing a young magician-in-training. His corruption did not stop at this point, but was ongoing. Having Dirty Dick saw a girl in half—an involuntary assistant—with a rusty chainsaw during a magic show was Ovid's limit, marking that point at which an author knows it is not just pornography, but downright filth and corruption that is occupying his work.

But Ovid found that trying to control his writing in any way brought about inaction, total paralysis. Ovid thought, "Why can't I just do a traditional romantic or dramatic story? Why not a variation on a classic script—a *Casablanca* for today's public, with that Bogart guy saying 'I'm looking at you, kid' and 'A man and a woman don't amount to a hill of dirt in this crazy world'?" (It's a good thing Ovid didn't say this aloud, as his blatant misquotation might stir up an angry mob of *Casablanca* fans.)

Wanting only to author a book about nobility and loss, Ovid would hold back with his work on a suspicion that his imagination was totally corrupt. Contrary to his ambitions of writing a romantic story, his actual plots had an inclination toward sin and iniquity of biblical proportion, but as if updating a story of Sodom and Gomorrah and not, say, that of a Good Samaritan.

Concluding that this bias toward immorality in his own fiction was totally out of his conscious control, Ovid had to obtain a warrant for "willful misconduct" from his company, OuLiPoCorp, by downloading an application, filling it out, and submitting it to a chairman. According to OuLiPoCorp's company policy, anything bad, or slightly naughty, had to pass strict scrutiny by a board of priggish schoolmarms.

Awaiting its approval, Ovid found distraction in a book by Franz Kafka, about a man on trial for nothing in particular, which took him about a month to finish.

Watching him go through this book at a snail's gait, Alyssa could not sit still. "Dad, didn't you go to Harvard?" Alyssa said.

"I did," Ovid said, without looking up from his book, "long ago."

"So how is it that you can't blow through a book that long in a day?"

"Skimming books wasn't a part of our curriculum, I don't think," said Ovid.

"Obviously not," said Alyssa. "You should try Vladimir Nabokov. *Lolita* will blow your mind, no joking."

Ovid had to work to contain his passing discomfort. "Instructors assign *Lolita* in high school now?" Ovid said. "For what class?"

"No, I took it up on my own, just for fun," said Alyssa.

Ovid, thought, *That again! Just for fun. It's always 'for fun' with this young crowd!*

"Writing is an awful liability, too—an onus to carry around with honor and humility—a gift from God." But backing away from this Puritan instinct, Ovid cut short this thought. "And what kind of a book is *Lolita*, would you say?"

"It's that kind of book that puts difficult truths right in front of you. That kind of book that taps into our cultural unconscious in a way not many can," said Alyssa.

"It's also corrupt, though, don't you think? A man has his way with a young girl who is practically his own child. What kind of rot is that? Any fool could think up such disgusting stuff." Ovid was hoping to dismiss this topic by waving his hand, as though shooing away a fly.

"I think that's his point, Dad, that all of us *do* think up this disgusting stuff, but don't confront it in our own souls. You and I opt to look upon our souls as without a stain, and favor an approach of vilifying such a passion as ugly and wholly Satanic. Though what is finally torn down by such an approach is not *this* passion—as it is an inclination within us as old as Cro-Magnon man—but all passion, and with it, our humanity."

Ovid sat through a long, awkward gap in his and Alyssa's talk, without so much as a murmur.

"I'm glad I got your analysis of Nabakov's work. Now go finish your schoolwork," said Ovid, who, in a twist of family dynamics, found it was now Alyssa who was thinking too much, and about such disturbing things. Ovid, by contrast, was sick of thinking anything at all, and was waiting for his application to pass, so his own smutty book could go on.

BOOK TWO

First Part

You probably grasp at this point that Ovid's world was not an ordinary world (as Durand Durand's was not an ordinary world). But far from growing numb to this fact, Ovid was too in touch with his pain not to mark how his world was spinning and dissolving, as if in a tornado. "How can OuLiPoCorp insist on insuring 'willful misconduct' for having immoral thoughts? How is it that a man could drop out of a blank gray sky, and nobody thought anything of it? How did Alyssa abruptly turn into a book critic without warning, and how did my own conduct turn from that of an innocuous British man-child into that of a lascivious old man?"

"This world must contain a grand cosmic irony," thought Ovid, "that I cannot fathom with only fifty rotations around a small star, on a boundary of a distant galaxy in what astronomy calls our 'Milky Way.'

"But who, finally, is laughing at all of this? If it is all a big gag aiming at our human folly, what god is coordinating this production, in all its intricacy, and its convincingly random organic activity? Who is mocking us with his dark, cryptic brand of humor?"

What a quandary for our protagonist to find awaiting him at this crossroads in his biography. Doubt was always plaguing Ovid, but this kind of agnosticism was continuous, unbound. Ovid could, if Ovid saw fit, put his inquiry to God, and pray all day, and still find no solution. Not born into a spiritual community (Anglicanism is hardly a robust spiritual philosophy), Ovid could not falsify a faith. But Ovid *was* curious about what was to follow this span of days—this mortal captivity, or *Maya*, as Buddhists call it.

Most of all, Ovid had this wish: to know if man had an autonomous will, or was bound to karma, circling through a thousand incarnations of his soul. Hinduism, Buddhism, Judaism, Christianity, and Islam all had ways of satisfying this longing for immortality. But, though Ovid did think a spiritual foundation was important, no path sought by any individual custom struck him as *most pious* or as *unmistakably holy* by comparison. Nothing stood out intrinsically as "God's words."

Rummaging around his study now, Ovid was sorting books and art prints, thinking about all his past associations with this stuff. This map of Australia was a gift from Lily—a girl whom Ovid was dating prior to shacking up with Anna—who took up cartography as a hobby, and who thought it would look intriguing to Ovid that, down in Oz, a map of our world is longitudinally backwards (that is, making it so that, on a compass, south is pointing up, and north is pointing down), so that Australia is on top, and Canada is on bottom (which is fitting, Ovid thought).

Ovid also found a monograph by Harry Math, who was at Harvard with Ovid back in sixty-six. At Harvard, Ovid was half as old as any boy or girl in his class. Harry Math was angry at Ovid for his youth. Harry would always say of him, during a writing workshop, "I think Ovid has raw ability, but his work lacks polish." And Ovid, only a kid (and a crybaby at that), would always say, "Waaaah!"

Harry wound up titling his first book *Sorrows of Young Ovid*, in a sly admonition of Ovid. In Harry's book, this protagonist—a suicidal young man—is full of ambition, but fails to attain his lofty goals for lack of that quality by which a man soars, or falls: grit. Harry's "Ovid" falls for a woman, "Anna," who is stunning, but shallow. In his passion for "Anna," "Ovid" is blind to "Anna's" obvious pining for "Harry," a dashing suitor whom "Anna" will finally marry, upon that book's sorrowful conclusion: "Ovid" blows his own brains out.

In addition to this curious work, Ovid found a print of a painting by Wassily Kandinsky, a stack of old compact discs of Bartok, and thirty books by Balzac. Such a worldly man was young Ovid! So promising! Such glorious aspirations!

All this cultural rubbish, wasting away in a brick building on an outskirt of Madison, Wisconsin. What to do with it all? Throw it away?

Disturbing this train of thought was a fax from OuLiPoCorp:

To Applicant (Ovid Dullann):

CanonicaLit, Inc., through its subsidiary OuLiPoCorp, must ask for additional information from said applicant, apropos of his inquiry into a warrant for willful misconduct.

First you must add six digits to your staff ID, which right now has only four digits. Staff ID is usually shown in this format: xx-xxxxx-xxx. In fact, your digitation throughout this application is full of flaws.

Also, narrow your account of said misconduct to a thousand words. Do not furnish a summary of your story, as it cannot grant us anything but an inkling of what your story is about. Or, if you can, simply attach a copy of Dirty Dick's Sick Mystic Tricks, or what part of it you can finish by tomorrow."

Yours truly,
Administration Official #6246

"So, OuLiPoCorp wants my book!" said Ovid aloud, to nobody in particular, "I shoulda' known." Paranoia was as natural to Ovid as a madman acting out his monomaniacal fantasy—as intrinsic as Ahab following Moby-Dick from Atlantic to Pacific coasts, down into fathoms unknown. And Anna, poor Anna, was his Starbuck, sinking along with him, drowning in Ovid's insanity, out of dumb loyalty.

In fact, Anna was, in that instant, swimming in Konstantinos' pool (that pool which was also a cushion for Ovid's fall), chatting with Anzora about how *difficult* husbands can act on occasion. Not sinking or drowning, as Ovid thought, but floating along, looking up at a swirl of stars, rapt in a mood of calm that Anna's husband, in his paranoia, could not possibly fathom.

Sitting in his study, Ovid was again struck with a conviction that an amorphous thing in his world was missing—just as Ovid had thought that Durand Durand's lipogram was lacking, and just as Ovid had known (from his kids' discussion) that *nothing* was casting a shadow on his world, so Ovid was now struck with this notion: that his own past was simply a story "told by an idiot, full of sound and fury, signifying nothing."

And Ovid was hit by a conundrum: By which idiot was his own story told? As you know, a habitual agnosticism did not allow Ovid any possibility of a God. "But," Ovid thought, "indisputably, a kind of natural or spiritual body—an Author of all my worldly affairs—is writing out my history, animating my body, and guiding all my actions." But who? Which author was writing out his story? Ovid was paging through a glossary in his *Who's Who in Authorship*, looking for an author who fits this sort of narration.

"Not Tobias Wolff, nor Virginia Woolf; not Thomas nor any wolf. Not Virgil, naturally, or any Roman (including that original Ovid). Rick Moody, author of 'Boys'? Jamaica Kincaid, author of 'Girl'?" Ovid couldn't say.

"What about Thomas Pynchon? *Gravity's Rainbow* was funny, absurd, and hard to wrap my mind around. And I'd always thought that OuLiPoCorp had its own Laszlo Jamf, conditioning my mind as an infant, as Jamf did with Slothrop. Oh, but this author's habit for obscurity and allusion is no match for Pynchon's.

"What about that famous Italian author, Italo Calvino, who would publish fantastical yarns about a viscount who got cut in half; or a suit of armor that thinks it is an actual knight of an actual kingdom; or a baron who quits his land-bound world to pass his nights lying among boughs of oak that span a broad swath of land?

"Is Italo Calvino my author?" Ovid thought aloud, knowing that many of Calvino's books had populations containing only consonants, such as Qwfwq, Vhd Vhd, Xlthx, and so on, so that his own associations with such odd folks as Durand Durand, Konstantinos Diamantaras, Harry Math, and Raymond Q would not stand out as so totally absurd.

But no. Italo Calvino was not living in 2004. Nor was Ovid's world so basically Italian that it could pass as a work of Calvino's. His own world was dark—a world in which a romantic but suicidal autistic man drops to his doom, in which a man's writing is too disturbing for his own liking, in which a ridiculously playful author was going around this world substituting God's will with his own.

This quandary was so troubling to Ovid that our protagonist was succumbing again to his insomnia. It was not that Ovid could not lay down for a nap, but that Ovid was always waking up, always conscious, his mind racing impossibly fast, too fast for his body to catch up. A constant pulsation in his cranium, a rapid thump-thump of blood and oil sloshing around in his skull, as if his circulatory organ was doing what his brain should.

Part Two

That night, a visitation from a ghost—or a hallucinatory symptom of his psychosis—told Ovid all about his quandary of authorship, and about Ovid's mission in this world.

Ovid was sorting through his books, arranging all his works of fiction by color and width of binding. Out of a haphazard stack of writing manuals, inclining from a wall, a shadowy librarian with a flowing cloak sprang forth, clad in chains, irons clinking around his wrists. This gaunt, thin form, rising up from a mountain of books, brought to mind a volcano spouting ash and lava. But, far from spouting lava, this gray ghost said unto Ovid, "I am a ghost of Christmas past," adding hastily, "But don't you try and run off."

Ovid had always thought that talk of ghosts was so much humbug, and Ovid was particularly wary of stuffy, British librarian phantoms. "But... I don't *know* you," said Ovid dubiously. "Shouldn't a ghost go haunt his old antagonists, out of an old spiritual animosity?"

"Absurd!" said this smoky wraith. "Ghosts don't haunt maliciously. A ghost simply inhabits a domain, and owns it by haunting out any riffraff. This is *my* library, which only I haunt."

"But it is *my* study," Ovid said, contrarily.

That ghost was riding on air as though swimming, straining with its limbs just to stay afloat. "It is your study right now, but it was my library long ago... and it still *is*, if you catch my drift." In that instant a wind drift did, in fact, blow into Ovid's study through a window—a drift that Ovid caught.

If this is truly a ghost librarian, thought Ovid, opportunistically, *it may hold a solution to my quandary of authorship.*

Changing tactics, Ovid put his acting mask on. "As a ghost, and as a librarian, you must know many things," Ovid said, in a blatantly sycophantic way.

"Oh, I do. I am a virtual dictionary of information. What do you want to know?" said that ghost librarian to Ovid.

Ovid was struggling to put his inquiry *just so.* "Is an author writing out my history, animating my body, and guiding all my actions?" Ovid finally said.

It took all his might for this ghost-librarian to lift his arm and point out of Ovid's study window. "Look," Ghost of Christmas Past said.

Why is it, you might ask, that Durand Durand, Konstantinos Diamantaras, and now Ghost of Christmas Past, would all call upon Ovid to "Look"? Is Ovid lacking in vision? It is so. But, alas, no ophthalmologist can assist him in that sort of vision that Ovid lacks.

And what is that blank spot on top of his ophthalmologist's chart, anyway?

Looking out of his north-facing wall, Ovid saw his own first Christmas as a boy: a tidy flat in London, a rich family, a hot toddy and a cinnamon stick, four stockings hanging up on a.... *Why four?* Ovid thought. *I was born an only child.* To his shock and dismay, Ovid saw that, in addition to his mom and dad, a third adult was sharing this Christmas Day with him as a baby: a woman who was obviously flirting with both Mr. and Mrs. Dullann. Was *this* what Ovid's mom and dad did all throughout his childhood, taking in wild animals and "having a go" on his living room sofa? As Ovid thinks back to his youth, Ovid brings to mind a long list of "aunts" that his folks would bring in for a month or two, but who always wound up vanishing at midnight on a Sunday. Ovid always found it odd that his dad paid his Aunt Molly fifty pounds a day just to sit on his lap and sing to him.

But Baby Ovid thinks up a good psychological tool to avoid this truth: "Look, Mommy! I'm a musician!" Baby Ovid, at just thirty months old, stands up and walks up to his family's grand piano. Starting to play, Baby Ovid bursts forth with a basic two-chord harmony, using both of his hands. How promising! What an auspicious start for a musical prodigy!

"That's all right, baby," Ovid's mom says, starting to kiss that third adult, that Nobody-Knows-Who, acting amorous in front of Ovid in a way that both draws in and disgusts him.

Picking up a paintbrush, Baby Ovid coats a blank canvas with a portrait of tall shadows subtly fusing into an inky black octopus. "Look, Daddy! I'm an artist!" Though his painting is disturbing, its maturity is striking—not what you'd think of a thirty-month-old child coming up with on his own. Will Ovid go into visual arts? What is Ovid promising us now?

"Why don't you go and draw in your room?" Ovid's dad said, pushing his son into a tall, looming hallway with dim lights and hardwood floors. Turning around, Ovid is lost. His family's flat is a labyrinth, so big and out of proportion that it could pass as a kingdom of giants. Ovid is wary of walking down a big, scary hallway without company, so sits down and, out of natural curiosity, looks through a crack in his living room doorway.

Ovid's dad sat around in a Santa Claus outfit all morning, but strips off his pants and boots now, walking around top-half Santa, bottom-half Santa Junior. Ovid will not stick around to watch what Mrs. Dullann and Nobody-Knows-Who do with Santa Claus and his dangling mini-Santa.

Moving to his family library, Ovid picks out a book and starts in: "It was a bright cold day in April...." Just noticing this uncanny ability to look at any word and say it aloud instantly, Ovid shouts out, "Mommy! Daddy! I am a smart boy! I am a smart boy!" But Pinocchio has nobody to applaud his trans-formation. From his family's common room, sounds of huff-ing and groaning and pounding, as though a fat man is doing jumping jacks on his living room sofa.

Ovid walks down to his living room to find out what all this fuss is about. Not a fat man, as it turns out, but an animal "with two backs," or, on this occasion, two backs plus Nobody-Knows-Who's back.

Post-coitus, this bacchanalian trio lazily sighs, lying in a shiny pool of skin. Pulling out a joint, passing it around and puffing away, a musky odor quickly fills this room, and Ovid walks in and just stands, with his chin down.

"Ovid, baby. Flip on that TV, won't you?" Nobody-Knows-Who says. "Your aunt wants to watch *Andy Griffith*."

Trying at first to put on an *Andy Griffith* play, but failing to act out his part as young Lil' Taylor to his dad's satisfaction (Ovid is naturally a Don Knotts, and not a Ron Howard), and having his mom shout at him for "acting a fool," Ovid would bow out, and dutifully click on his duo-color TV, sit back, and watch.

As his "family" sat around focusing all thought upon this box of twinkling lights, Ovid found a roach clip with a joint still burning down, and put it to his mouth, puffing thirstily as a kid suckling milk from a nanny goat.

Fading out, this vision of Christmas Past lost its hold upon Ovid, subsiding into an ordinary sight: a frosty window on a cold day.

"That was gratuitous," Ovid said. "I know just as much now about my quandary as I did a half an hour ago."

"Not so," said Ghost of Christmas Past. "You know much now that you did not, which is only starting to form in your mind.... But I will find a solution to your inquiry. So... you want to know if an author is writing out your history, animating your body, guiding all your actions?"

"I do," said Ovid.

Ghost of Christmas Past got up on a stool and took out a card. This ghost librarian was so old that it did not know anything about computing or surfing or CD-ROMs, or any of a googol ways in which you or I might go hunting for information. So Ghost of Christmas Past had to physically walk to a card catalog, climb up a stool, and pull out a card with information on it. With his own hands!

"What's it say?" Ovid said.

"This card will point us to a book, and in that book, a paragraph, and within that paragraph, a word—just a word—solving, finally, this quandary of yours," said Ghost of Christmas Past, looking oddly whimsical.

But it turns out that finding this particular book is an arduous task, occupying two full hours, as Ghost of Christmas Past took apart Ovid's study book by book, stopping to laugh at a particularly unworthy book, such as a *Hardy Boys*, from his boyhood days, or to skim a book that was in print posthumous to his passing away (during Lyndon Johnson's administration). In particular, Ghost of Christmas Past could not put down a

Dutch translation of *Schlachthof-Funf*, in which a World War II grunt, Billy Pilgrim, is unstuck from all rationality, until his assassination by Paul Lazzaro, following his abduction by Tralfamadorians and involuntary cohabitation with porn-star Montana Wildhack.

Finally, just as Ovid was about to throw up his hands and walk off, Ghost of Christmas Past said, "I found it!"

"What is it?" said Ovid, anxiously turning around.

Ovid saw Ghost of Christmas Past flipping through a hard-bound book, stopping halfway through it and staring down, as though about to fall in.

"I can confirm that an author is writing out your history, animating your body, and guiding your actions," it said, looking up.

"Who?" Ovid said, but by now, this ghost was growing dim, dissipating, as if a fog had blown in through his north-facing window.

"I cannot say. But I will say this: that Ovid is not a man with a job, and bills to pay, and obligations to his family. Ovid is a participant in this world, and must go and do that for which a man is born." Having said that, Ovid's ghost librarian did vanish into a mist.

"Which is what?" said Ovid, frantically, wanting to hold on to this illusion, but knowing its futility. "Which is what?... For what function is a man born into this world?"

Third Part

Ovid was conscious, now, of an author writing out his history, animating his body, and guiding his actions. Walking out from his library into broad daylight, our protagonist was at this point waking up to a disturbing fact of his fictional individuality: that a high circulation among library patrons is important to survival. "If all my library-going public abruptly put down this book," Ovid thought, "I would not go on living. With nobody to watch my goings-on in this world, my story would stop short, in an unfulfilling conclusion."

Just skydiving, party-going, and applying for a warrant for willful misconduct to author a smutty book is scant action for a story, Ovid thought. "I must go and do things that all humanity wants to know about. I must, as that ghost librarian said, 'do that for which a man is born.'" His mission was now taking on a particular form. Ovid was planning to go off in pursuit of unknown horizons, to grasp his human condition as much as a man humanly can, surviving by acting, without thought, for as long as Ovid could.

"I must run away," Ovid thought, "to satisfy my public. And most of all, OuLiPoCorp must not obtain my book!"

But how to clarify this for Anna? Anna was always hanging from a promontory, always about to fall into a canyon of alcoholism which had no bottom. Could Ovid's flight bring about Anna's fall?

And, supposing Anna was not at risk of falling off a wagon, and was just as cool and calm as Anna put across, could such a woman, so pragmatic and rational, actually grasp what convolutions it took to attain this insight? Would Anna think that this is of his imagination only, and say, "I'm sorry, Ovid, but this fantasy has no truth in it. No author is writing out your history, animating your body, and guiding all your actions." Would Anna play a spoilsport to Ovid's paranoid wing-nut conspiracy?

Ovid thought that such fumbling toward a clarification could only confound Anna, and mystification was not what Ovid had in mind. Ovid was not about to confront Anna on a war footing. So his plan of attack was obvious: total withdrawal of his troops.

That night, Ovid did nothing but wait until 2 a.m., upon which hour Ovid snuck downstairs, through a hallway, out of his front door, running away from his family, just as Ovid ran away for his skydiving trip, as Ovid was always running away. But as Ovid was crawling into his Toyota, Ovid saw Alyssa sitting right in front of him, turning an ignition switch on his pickup.

"What's going on?" Ovid said, looking timid, not knowing if Alyssa was catching him in mid-flight or if Ovid was catching Alyssa taking his truck out for an illicit midnight outing. Alyssa instantly *got it*: Ovid had a bag slung around his arm and was taking off for unknown horizons, just as Alyssa was.

"Dad, I'm running away, too," Alyssa said.

"Why would you do that?" Ovid said, handily ignoring that such was his own plan, too.

"It's Aaron," Alyssa said with a sigh. "I can't stand living as his twin. It's frustrating. It's as though Aaron, by only doing what all boys do—putting up a photograph of a fantasy girl in his room, masturbating to it constantly, not wiping it up, thinking nobody knows about it—is turning our world into a Y-chromosomal match of paintball, in which only Aaron has a gun. I just can't act in my usual capacity as a twin—such as bonding in an almost psychic way, as two siblings sharing a womb do. And I can't just mimic an ignorant girl who knows nothing about boys. I know his mind too thoroughly, but it's as if Aaron isn't as conscious of my own mind. Aaron is in his own world, losing touch with what is around him."

Ovid, falling back into his patrimonial habit, said, "Darling. I wouldn't turn Aaron into a lab rat—a thing to pick apart and study using your psychological toolbox. Boys go through difficult things, and girls go through difficult things distinct from boys. Aaron is splitting from you; Aaron is growing, and might not want to stay bound to his family throughout high school. It's normal; trust Daddy on this. You should stick around, just for now. How about it?"

"C'mon, Dad," Alyssa said, signaling to him, "I'm gonna go, with or without you. So why don't you tag along?"

Among this car's junk was a toy Yoda, a *Star Wars* doll, hanging from its mirror. As I said, Ovid was a film buff, and a Cold War sci-fi fan. Now Ovid was looking up at his toy Yoda, simply out of distraction, but found in this plastic plaything a fountain of wisdom. "Just as in *Star Wars*," Ovid thought, "as Anakin's twins' survival was brought about by dividing up this pair at birth, so too is a division of our twins from us a vital act toward guarding Aaron and Alyssa against my corruption."

Ovid was imagining a distant day in which Darth Ovid, a Sith Lord with intimidating black armor and ominous-sounding inhalations, plots to corrupt his own kids into ruling this world along with him. Taking his fantasy too far, Ovid saw his amoral (but unavoidably cool) stand-in using his choking ability to finish off his own assistant, saying, "I find your lack of faith disturbing," just as an original Darth villain says it in *Star Wars*.

With this thought in mind, taking action to guard Alyssa was but a fait accompli. "You can run away," said Ovid to Alyssa, "but not with your dad. You go your own way, and I go my way."

"No way," Alyssa said, it just now occurring to Alyssa how having Ovid along could assist this situation financially.

"I am issuing an ultimatum," said Ovid. "You can't go along. I'm going far away from Madison. Just find your own path, and follow it without going astray, or you risk losing your way." Ovid was almost crying again—that's two occasions, by my count, in as many days. "I want you to attain all your goals in this world."

But this oration, far from inspiring Alyssa to go off and "do that for a which a woman is born," as it did Ovid, brought Alyssa back to this conclusion: I should follow Ovid if I don't want to run out of cash by tomorrow.

Anyway, Ovid's surprising frailty, and his sympathy for Alyssa's difficulty, stood in contrast to how Ovid was through-out Alyssa's childhood, and it did allow Alyssa to look upon him as human, not just an aloof patriarch with a habit for ran-dom acts of art-making, and an occasional saving quality.

"I'm coming with you, Daddy," was all Alyssa said, and Ovid ("Daddy"!) could not possibly go against Alyssa's wish.

Part Four

If Alyssa is coming along on my mission, Ovid thought, *who will I run away from now?* Taking a highway south through Illinois, Missouri, and Arkansas, Ovid did not stop in Chicago or St. Louis. Urbanity and its comforts did not pull on Ovid—at root a country boy who had originally thought of staying in Wisconsin until his final days, particularly in Madison, which was too small to call a big city, but too big to call a small town. Purporting to follow his road atlas toward a mid-Atlantic coast—which vicinity was Virginia, Maryland, North and South Carolinas— Ovid was actually going south, to swampland.

Ovid was trying to act sporadically—anticipating that which was normal for him and not doing it—to trick his Author (who was following him, cataloguing his actions, taking down data, dictating all his motions through this country) into mistaking his plans for a vacation. To distract his Author, Ovid was chit-chatting with Alyssa about this and that. "So what was your plan? To what distant lands had you thought of going, with a tank full of gas, with no grownups to hold you back, and with—"

"—with my dad in tow?" said Alyssa, who was finishing his syntactical constructions now.

"No. I was going to say, 'and with a boy's arm around your waist'?" said Ovid.

"No, Dad. I'm still a virgin," Alyssa said.

"Naturally," Ovid said, smirking proudly that his baby girl thought that having an arm around your waist was tantamount to losing your virginity.

"I wouldn't do anything with a boy anyway," Alyssa said, which Ovid took as a sign of his baby girl's purity, but was actually Alyssa imparting to him that Ovid's "baby girl" was not, in fact, drawn to boys.

"How about you?" Alyssa said. "Why did you want to run off so abruptly?"

Pausing, taking air into his lungs, Ovid said, "I had a vision. And in this vision, a ghost said, 'Ovid is not a man with a job, and bills to pay, and obligations to his family. Ovid is a participant in this world, and must go and do that for which a man is born."

"Which is what?" said Alyssa.

"It didn't say," said Ovid, caught up in a nostalgia for things impossibly lost.

"That sucks," Alyssa said. "What an annoying vision."

Ovid almost forgot that Alyssa wasn't an adult, and thinks as a child thinks. "You could say that," said Ovid, finally.

"So what is our final goal, as far as a location?" Alyssa said.

"My plan is to go to Australia, actually, but for now, I just want to tour our good ol' U.S. of A. First stop: Washington, D.C., our national capitol!" Ovid, as you know, was misinforming Alyssa, to conduct his Author along a wrong path—to point him astray—so that Ovid might vanish from his radar (which didn't work). "I was also thinking of Florida. Or California! You know, a bit of sun down in La La Land."

"If you had a 'vision' that said you should go off and do 'that for which a man is born,' why would you want to go visit popular landmarks, as a tourist?"

"You don't want to go to L.A.?" said Ovid.

"I might go to San Francisco, but not L.A. No way." Alyssa was hinting again, bringing up San Francisco.

"OK, OK. California is out," said Ovid. "To Florida!"

For an hour or so, Ovid was driving on, staring straight in front of him at a long, blank span of road. "What is it that D.C. stands for?" said Alyssa abruptly.

"District of Columbia," said Ovid.

"Why *Columbia*? Is Washington, D.C. actually part of Columbia?" said Alyssa. Just Ovid's luck. His child was finally asking him about national history, and Ovid was at a loss for what to say.

"Don't talk crazy. Columbia is a country way down south, caught up in a constant civil war, known for both its cocoa and its coca," Ovid said. Noticing that Alyssa was sulking, Ovid said, "What's on your mind?"

"Nothing," Alyssa said instinctually, but actually, Alyssa was full of things to say—things that ordinarily Alyssa was happy to bury, to stow away for an unknown day of total, uncompromising validation for all abnormality.

"I'm a man," Alyssa said, finally announcing what Alyssa was subtly communicating to Ovid all day.

"I think I would know if my baby girl was born a boy," said Ovid. "What you want to say is, 'I'm gay.'"

"No, Dad. I'm not gay. I am a man… within," said Alyssa. "From now on, you must say 'him' and 'his' to show that you honor my manhood. Masculinity is an important part of who I am."

"But, darling, it's OK to look for intimacy with a woman as a woman," said Ovid. "You can't rightly say that your body is that of a man." As Alyssa's body was growing full into womanhood, Ovid could not but mark how his baby girl was almost an adult, and it was disturbing to him to think that this physical maturation was, to Alyssa, a malformation.

"I know that. Why is it so difficult to grasp that I am a man? Aaron is my twin, and Aaron is a man," Alyssa said.

"Aaron is just a boy," said Ovid, nitpicking now. Sighing, Ovid said, "I support your attraction to girls; I am sympathizing with you, in fact, as I know what an awful thing it is to harbor an attraction to girls, who may not harbor an attraction for you…." Alyssa was looking oddly at Ovid, who was rambling now. "But, by chromosomal fact, darling, you must admit, it looks as though Alyssa is stuck with Alyssa."

Alyssa was sulking. "A gay man in a woman's body has an attraction to a man, and a straight man in a woman's body has an attraction to a woman. Got it?"

"I'm sorry, it's just so confusing," Ovid said.

"All right, I'll switch around who I am just to simplify things for you," Alyssa said sarcastically.

Ovid was stumbling with his words, trying to put forward a lucid thought. "I don't know why this is causing such rancor. I support you. I'm only saying that a woman is a biological fact; picking and choosing has nothing to do with it."

"Why do you insist on maintaining a position on a topic you know nothing about?" Alyssa said.

"I know what it is to go through this world as a man," said Ovid, his words fading to nothing.

Until stopping at a Holiday Inn in Arkansas, not a word was said about Alyssa's finding his inmost soul—his manhood.

Conspicuously awkward, Ovid put on his car radio, tuning in to a country music station. Luckily, it was playing classic country: Hank Williams, say, with only a small portion of Garth Brooks. Ovid wasn't into country music at all, but as his trip took him down south, Ovid found a growing admiration for country music stars, cowboy hats and all. Now that, in Arkansas, Ovid could not avoid country music, its poignancy struck Ovid as full of import, including songs that Ovid had, until now, thought of as sappy and maudlin.

At this Holiday Inn—a standard off-highway lodging—a "No Vacancy" sign was now lit up. This pair of Dullanns was its last admission that night. Out of a window of his room, Ovid saw a glowing pink flamingo sign, a row of pickup trucks, and a group of hoodlums smoking what was probably marijuana, lighting match upon match and allowing it to burn down to its nub, charring a thumb or two of this town's local thug population. Turning his focus back indoors, watching his prodigal son drifting off, somnambulating upon a plaid quilt, languorously sighing away a day of dissatisfaction, without so much as fluffing a pillow, Ovid thought how his offspring was not so bad. Alyssa *was* a man, Ovid thought, or this is what a man should aim for.

It was both gratifying and disappointing for Ovid to watch how Alyssa's young adulthood was unfolding. Not many in this world know with such conviction what color our soul is. Now that Alyssa had found his, it was surprisingly hard for Ovid to join him in this victory lap. Why? What was drawing him back, withholding his joy?

It was this: that a notional man hiding within an actual woman was just too absurd, too humorous a thought to admit. It was as though Ovid had found his way into a Monty Python skit—and not a savvy political parody, but a comic potshot, a low blow for lowbrow laughs—from its BBC program, *Monty Python's Flying Circus* (during his own childhood in London, Ovid would watch a lot of absurd British TV).

"Why should I think this way?" thought Ovid. "I'm a high-brow sort, with a broad mind about this kind of thing, and *Christ almighty*, this is my own daught... or... actually, my son that I'm talking about. I must honor Alyssa's wish, or risk losing his trust. As long as Alyssa is in my guardianship, his will is still my command."

This, anyway, was Ovid's working philosophy on that particular day.

Fifth Part

At 6 a.m., with dawn still advancing on Arkansas, Ovid lazily sat up and took out his road atlas, plotting his day out on a colorful map. Looking around his room, Ovid found it odd that Alyssa was not lying in his foldout cot, snoozing away till noon. Alyssa's bag was missing from its rung, and a pair of boots was missing, too; and Alyssa—if a faint floral aroma wafting in from his lavatory was any indication—had probably had a bath at an ungodly hour this morning.

Ovid quickly spun his blinds around to look out of this room's front window and, to his satisfaction, saw Alyssa sitting on a chair, porchbound, smoking a joint. This aroma was unmistakably *not* floral.

Out his door in a flash, Ovid was sitting across from his son. "So what did *you* do all morning?"

"This and that," Alyssa said cryptically. "Uh… I took up smoking," Alyssa had to add just to stop Ovid staring at him.

"Is that all?" Ovid said loudly. Although Ovid was skillful at hiding it, Ovid was livid.

"Why do you want to know?" Alyssa said.

"I just want to know what I'm up against. Do you always roll up a joint at dawn?" Ovid could not contain his opinions at this point.

"Uh-huh," said Alyssa, "And you know what? I don't worry about you and Mom finding out, 'cuz you work all day, and Mom is spacing out on Zoloft all morning."

"So… your smoking hash is all my fault?" Ovid said.

"Christ, Dad. It's just grass. It's not as though I'm smoking opium, or dosing on LSD. It's not as bad as drinking alcohol, which is what most kids do at my school," Alyssa said, with such rationality that it was hard for Ovid to contradict.

Ovid thought about how it was for him as a young man at Harvard—taking mushrooms and smoking marijuana (or any "natural" drug) with your morning biscuits was no big thing. In fact, Ovid took so much hash in his school days that his chums took to calling him "Cotton Mouth," on account of his constant thirst. Alyssa's way of acting out was, Ovid had to admit, mild by comparison.

"All right," Ovid said, pulling up a chair. "I want a puff."

"Cool," said Alyssa, assuaging Ovid's nagging suspicion that smoking up with his son was not a good thing for a dad to do. Contrarily, it was what brought Ovid and Alyssa back into harmony again.

Soon, both Dullanns sunk into a fit of convulsions worthy of a grand mal fit. Slap-happy and punch-drunk, this pair couldn't think straight without going all curvy again in a paroxysm of mock joy.

Ovid could not stop giggling. "Is that a hobbit? Or is that man just far away?" Ovid said, stifling a laugh. Actually, a small man *was* rapidly approaching, walking up a flight of stairs.

"Hi, how'r you?" said this Tom Thumb, with a slight slur, as any dwarf might do—as did Tattoo from *Fantasy Island*, to whom this man *did* look distinctly similar.

"I am truly high. And how high'r you?" Ovid said, also with a slight slur, as any pot-smoking nitwit would do.

This man, whom Ovid mistook for a munchkin out of Frank L. Baum's *Wizard of Oz*, was not in as humorous a mood as Ovid, and stood by watching him stoically. Soon this man had caught Alyssa up in a dialog, chatting back and forth about who knows what. For Ovid was busy picturing Alyssa as Judy Garland in Dorothy drag, and this guy as Munchkinland Mayor. If so, who was Ovid in all of this? A cowardly lion? A tin woodsman? Toto, possibly? His only conclusion was this: Ovid was *not* in Kansas. Ovid was in *Arkansas*.

"Did you know that, if you put on a Pink Floyd album as you watch *Wizard of Oz*, it will run in sync with it, as a kind of soundtrack for that film?" Ovid said, as though his two companions could psychically follow his circuitous paths of thought.

"I'm sorry," said Alyssa, timidly, "my dad is totally out of it. I think this is his first joint in many, many moons."

Of sound mind now, noticing an abrupt shift in his situation, Ovid said "Hi," to this tiny man. Turning to Alyssa, Ovid said, audibly, "How do you know this guy?"

"I was talking to him this morning. Duh." Alyssa cast a look of apology at this aspiring inhabitant of Lilliput. (Ovid did fancy for an instant that his Author was Jonathan Swift, and Ovid was puzzling out how his story could pass as a satirical social criticism.) "Dad, this is Paco, from room forty-two. Paco is my supply guy. Paco is also going to Florida."

"Ah-haaaah!" said Ovid, still high, and paranoid as usual. Both Alyssa and Paco cast funny looks in Ovid's vicinity. "Following us, is that it?"

"Not at all," said Paco plainly, "I'm visiting my Aunt in Miami."

"Do you hail from Cuba originally?" Ovid said, thinking of a way to find Paco at fault for our botching up Bay of Pigs Invasion, for Cuba's crisis of '62, and for JFK's assassination.

Ignoring him now, Paco and Alyssa had a long talk about Florida and its islands, about immigration law, about Latinx history, and Florida's substantial Hispanic voting bloc. Alyssa took this opportunity to put to Paco his inquiry about why our nation's capital city is in a District of *Columbia*.

"I think it has to do with Columbus, you know?" said Paco, shrugging. Alyssa, indignant at Columbus for killing so many Indians, was taking this opportunity to go into a long disquisition into colonial history, using a bastardization of historical and postcolonial criticism. (In addition to taking up Nabokov, Alyssa was now a fan of both Howard Zinn and Noam Chomsky.)

Sitting idly by, watching this poor homunculus chat up his

daugh—No! It was his *son!*—was frustrating to Ovid out of all proportion. Why did Alyssa insist on talking to this pygmy as Ovid stood by with nothing to say? Didn't Alyssa know what a panic Ovid was in, high out of his mind, with a rapidly shrinking Spaniard intruding upon his story?

"I am now officially Alyssa's crony," thought Ovid, "just a crusty old man awaiting dismissal." Ovid didn't usually mind acting as copilot in such an affair, but, as it was still ambiguous just what kind of affair it was, Ovid's frustration was at a boiling point, and his paranoia was soaring.

"OK," said Ovid, clapping his hands, "I don't want to disrupt our morning powwow, but a highway awaits."

"Hold up," Alyssa said. "Don't you want a muffin or two first? Paco says that this inn has a lobby downstairs with a damn good pastry cook."

"I own a pastry shop," Paco said, by way of clarification.

"I don't doubt," said Ovid, "that you'd know a good pastry if you had it. I'm just not up for it, though. You two go, and I'll finish packing." Ovid was lying. Ovid did want a muffin. But Ovid was also in a rush, and his paranoia was blaring as loudly as a car alarm at midnight.

"It's almost noon, and I had brunch this morning," said Paco to Alyssa, "but why don't *you* go down and try a pastry? I'll occupy your dad."

"No prob," said Alyssa with a nod. "I wouldn't want to miss out on a good muffin." And as fast as you could say "Lollipop Guild," Alyssa was on his way downstairs, and Ovid was in Paco's solitary company.

For almost half an hour, Ovid said nothing, but sat in his chair, finishing off his joint.

"Wait…," Paco said abruptly. "Don't I know you?"

"Sorry, it was a lousy introduction. I'm Ovid Dullann," said Ovid, putting out his hand.

Paco shook it. "No no no, not from just now. From your past…."

Ovid didn't know how to say it, but Ovid did not think it a possibility that Ovid actually ran into, and summarily forgot, such a small man.

"How about...," Paco said. "Wait a min.... Didn't you sign on as an organ donor?"

"What?" Ovid did not at all grasp what Paco was implying.

"Yup. *That's* how I know you. I had a city job in Madison as a young man. I was a DMV guy." Paco had a smirk on, which was causing havoc to Ovid's paranoia. "So... did you sign on as an organ donor, or not?"

"I don't... think so," was all that Ovid could say.

"You *did*! Now... I forgot... *which* organs did you sign off on?" Paco said, stroking his chin as though in profound thought. "I think... wasn't it your pulmonary organ? That organ to which all our organs hold fast, pumping blood and bringing air from your lungs to your brain?"

Ovid unconsciously put his right hand on his bosom.

"Or was it your brain? That's it! It was your brain!" Paco was moving in on him, and Ovid was backing up against a wall. Ovid couldn't say why this tiny man was so scary to him.

"Didn't you ask for a lobotomy? Is that what's missing? Now, what would you do with a brain, if you had it?" Ovid could only blink, suck in his lip, and swallow air.

"Which is it, Ovid? Tin man, or straw man?" Paco was virtually shouting now, and Ovid thought how all this commotion must sound to Alyssa downstairs, as though his dad was caught in a fracas with an imp.

"Hmmm.... It looks as though I'm just a cowardly lion," Ovid said, trying to calm his mood with humor. It was working, or so Ovid thought, as Paco took out a matchbook and lit up a cig with him.

"What is Ovid running away from?" Paco said, puffing out a proportionally tiny cloud. "Going off to Florida on a whim, taking Alyssa with him, stopping at night, nothing to do but run?"

"I'm not running away," Ovid said, "I am *looking* for an important thing."

"What thing? A Holy Grail? At an off-highway Holiday Inn in Arkansas?" Paco said.

"No," said Ovid, trying and failing again at articulating his vision. "It's a quiddity that I'm looking for."

"A quiddity? A quiddity of what?"

"I can't say. I only know that I start from within and spiral outward, making contact with humanity as much as I can, through words and art and music, struggling for what is significant, until I'm carrion for worms, and throughout it all, looking for a lasting truth to cling to. Call it God, or spirit, or a Holy Grail, but I call it a quiddity—a quiddity of living as a thinking animal."

"How Camus of you! I think I'll grant you an honorary diploma from my School of Thinking Too Much; a ThD, our most illustrious honorific; that is, a 'Doctor of Thinkology'," said Paco, grinning. Paco, Ovid saw, was quoting (or misquoting, as Ovid also will occasionally do) *Wizard of Oz*, in a baldly ironic allusion to that film.

"But you must grant this much: that an unsought-for soul is not worth having," said Ovid. "And this world around us is all a part of its pursuit."

"So, you think a grand wizard of Oz is hiding within a curtain, running it all, pulling your strings?" said Paco, who, advancing upon this cowardly lion, allowing his lips to curl in obvious disdain, finally laid out his cards: "I *know* who it is."

Alyssa was walking upstairs. Though Ovid's blood was rushing through him, blazing with warmth, bringing a pink tint to his skin, Ovid saw that Alyssa did not catch anything unusual in this sight: no public display of passion, no turmoil or imbroglio, no panic or horror, no fight or flight instinct. To Alyssa it was just a trivial chat: a colloquy with a dwarf, and not a nightmarish vision, out of *spiritus mundi,* troubling his sight.

"I am sorry, but I must abandon you now. I am on my way out," said Paco, slipping out so swiftly that Ovid had no opportunity to ask him what was going on, calling out, "Oh what a world! What a world!" as his form was diminishing into a far horizon.

"I brought you a muffin from downstairs, and an Orangina," said Alyssa, still not fully grasping Ovid's plight. "I know how you can't stand Coca-Cola."

His body was shaking but, to look strong in front of Alyssa, Ovid spun around with a calm look on his mug, and said, "Why don't you start driving, just until Louisiana?"

Part Six

Ovid had in mind to visit Konstantinos' ranch in Louisiana—a vacation spot with vast tracts of land and a big Tudor mansion (an uncommon sort of building south of Mason-Dixon, but which struck Konstantinos as accommodating to his visitors from up north). But its location, in Pillowtown, was so far from Arkansas that it was as good as flying off to Mount Olympus.

Ovid was in a funny sort of mood—an outgrowth both of smoking a bag of marijuana this morning and his run-in with a mini-Machia-villain. Trying to distract his mind from its natural paranoia, Ovid brought Alyssa back to an old topic. "So what should I call you from now on?" Ovid said.

"Huh?" Alyssa was driving now, and trying to maintain focus on a narrow asphalt road, far from any highway.

"Should I call you Alyssa? Or Alistair, or what?" said Ovid.

"No. Nothing. Say what you want. As long as I know who you want to talk to." Finishing with a shrug, Alyssa thought this topic was void of any additional possibility.

"That won't do. I usually call you 'baby girl,'" Ovid said. "What boy wants his dad to call him 'baby girl'?"

Alyssa was taciturn, hurt that his dad could abandon calling him "baby girl" so quickly, and start calling him "Alistair," of all things.

"I don't think I'm up for driving," said Alyssa. "Thanks for allowing it and all, but what if a cop caught us—"

"—and saw you driving a pickup truck down a dirt road with your dad riding shotgun?" Ovid was smiling patronizingly. "That's about as common a sight as a stray dog in Arkansas."

"I just don't want to go to jail this trip, if that's OK with you," said Alyssa, starting to slow down, doing forty now.

"So, paranoia's got you, too? You and I form a frightful pair." Ovid had a thought. "Wait... didn't that tiny guy from this morning work at a DMV?"

Alyssa had a funny look on. "What guy?" said this boy-within-a-girl. "I don't know of any 'tiny guy' from this morning."

Ovid was sitting totally still as an instant of cold, dark horror was crawling up his spinal cord.

"I'm just fucking with you, Dad! Wow. Now I know not to ply you with drugs. *Christ.*" Alyssa was laughing, but Ovid could only calm down partway.

"I'll start driving now," Ovid said, sounding only as normal as a paranoiac could.

Switching positions, playing musical chairs in this tight car, Alyssa and Ovid both had a pang of claustrophobia, and as his arm involuntarily hit against Yoda (dangling from his car mirror), Ovid in particular had doubts as to this trip's continuation.

As soon as Ovid was road-bound, Alyssa, riding shotgun in Ovid's Toyota, said, "I gotta go."

"I know. I'm going, I'm going," said Ovid, mistaking Alyssa's complaint. "No, I gotta *go* go," said Alyssa.

"As in go-go *dancing?*" Ovid said, just playing now.

Alyssa cast him a look.

"OK," said Ovid, pulling up to a patch of lilacs. "Just go and void in that bush."

"Void? Why not just call it 'pissing'?" said Alyssa, who was starting to find all of Ovid's locutions annoying. "I don't *void.*"

Ovid put up his hands. "It's not my fault. That's what doctors call it."

"Doctors also call shit *stool*, Dad. You gonna start saying *stool* now?" In fact, Ovid did usually call his BMs "stool."

"Can't I talk how I want to talk?" Ovid's facial color was turning pink again. "Is my high diction an obstruction to our communication?"

"It's not high diction, Dad; it's clinical talk. You always talk in this roundabout way… it's just stupid." Alyssa was raring for a fight, Ovid thought. Or Alyssa was just fighting off a bout of PMS.

"Go on," Ovid said, indicating a bunch of plants that was going to act as Alyssa's impromptu bathroom.

"I will," said Alyssa, hoisting his body out of Ovid's Toyota with a yank, and "taking a piss" by a blooming lilac bush. Squatting, not standing up.

Ovid didn't know if Alyssa's candor was good for him or not. Did it solidify his bond with his son? Or did it just turn Alyssa against him? That kind of talk is hard to go back on. Ovid had a lot to say too, but was locking his lips tightly so as not to impart any information to his Author.

But soon, Ovid and Alyssa found accord—a mutual pact

to say nothing at all until arriving in Pillowtown, which was still a long way off.

That night, arriving at 2 a.m., Ovid was drowsily going through all his motions without clarity or focus: parking his car, bringing Alyssa up to a vacant room, finding a couch for him to crash on. "This is just for tonight," Ovid thought. "I don't want our visit to turn into a full-blown occupation." But "just tonight" would turn into a month, and a month would turn into two months, and soon it was almost autumn.

This two-month-span was an infinity for Alyssa, who could not admit that a random and involuntary thought of Madison now was an occasion for fond nostalgia. Ovid, for his part, lost days tidying up, shopping, doing anything within his ability to maintain this mansion, not wanting to insult his unwitting host by turning it into an animal sanctuary.

Stylistically, this mansion was classical, with a flavor of pop art (though this flavor was, in Ovid's opinion, too sugary for continuous consumption). Its landscaping was without a fault, and a fig orchard, surrounding a pond of lotus blossoms, was lain across its backyard, sown into this land as harmoniously as a patchwork quilt, to form a dramatic vista from that mansion's widow's walk, which ran along its rooftop.

Soon Ovid could not say what day it was. August thirty-first? Is that right? Or is August a thirty-day month?

On a Sunday—a day with no significant pull for Ovid, who did not go to church and, growing up Anglican, was hardly Christian at all—a spiritual visitation struck. On this occasion, it was not a spirit from Christmas past, but from Christmas not-too-long-ago. Ovid was up on a widow's walk, taking air. It was just that kind of cold that could justify a cookout to ward off autumn's rapid approach. Alyssa was stirring charcoals in an outdoor grill, raising a black cloud of fog. And within this cloud of fog was a spiritual body, a ghost, rising up to Ovid's rooftop location.

"Why do you throw your days away picking up trash, as any maid could do for six dollars an hour?" it said, looming from a billow of thick, ashy smog.

"Who's that?" Ovid said, quaking in his boots.

"So, you forgot your old companion, Durand Durand?" it said.

"Durand Durand! It is your ghost!" Ovid was aghast, but paradoxically glad for a social visit. "How is it, you know, to not own a body?" Ovid was still in shock from his visitor's arrival, but most curious about what final lot awaits us all.

"You must not carry on this way," said Durand Durand.

"How's that?" said Ovid, doubtfully.

"You had a vow, to uphold my lipogrammatic spirit by writing out your own." Durand Durand was frowning, as any angry spirit would in such a situation.

"I did, but it was all trash—just atrocious, poisonous smut, all of it."

"You must find a topic that will satisfy your morbidity without dominating your work. You should not turn your work into a total monstrosity, but you cannot just *abandon* it."

Ovid was downcast. "I'm sorry, Durand. I thought I could, but I was wrong."

"Stop dicking around!" said Durand, surrounding Ovid with that fog, which had a distinct aroma of hot dogs and bratwurst. "Look!" And just as it was with Ghost of Christmas Past, Ghost of Christmas Not-Too-Long-Ago took hold of Ovid's mind and brought a vision into it....

Christmas of 2004: Durand Durand is having Christmas all on his own, but for a visit from his cousin, Tim Cratchit, who is hobbling around on a crutch, on account of his crippling disability. Tim is small and wan, struggling to do basic things such as put on his own socks, a sight that instantly brings about Ovid's sympathy, inciting pity in him.

This two-room ranch has a brick foundation and cracking gray paint upon its walls. Durand Durand pulls down two stockings (his own dirty socks), full of just fruit and nuts. But for Tim Cratchit, Durand Durand's gift of sugar plums and almonds brings him Christmas joy. A pot of hot cocoa is starting to boil, and a stack of wood brings instant warmth to his domain.

Durand Durand, Ovid saw only now, was poor and insignificant: a lowly twig on a minor branch of OuLiPoCorp's giant oak, which was privy to blow off at any hint of a wind. To fall down into a patch of grass, and to try and avoid having his body split in two by Ovid's footprint on his way up, was Durand Durand's most promising option.

In fact, within months, on a skydiving trip with his boss at OuLiPoCorp, Durand Durand would snap.

Ovid's vision, part two, spun away on a cloud of fog, and with it, Durand Durand, a Ghost of Christmas Not-Too-Long-Ago.

"You don't truly think you can fool this fool into thinking that Tim Cratchit was your visitor on Christmas," Ovid rang out, angry at such blatant manipulation. "You didn't pass around sugar plums to your tiny, crutch-bound kinsman. Tiny Tim isn't your cousin!"

"No. But still… You must not go on as you do, or you will risk a similar ruin to my own." Durand Durand was fading, flowing upward, dissipating.

"Wait!" said Ovid, not knowing what to say, but not wanting Durand to go. Inviting Durand Durand to join in this outdoor grill, Ovid said, "Don't spirits go hungry in limbo, with no food or drink or anything?"

Nodding, Durand Durand said, "Hungry as a wolf," dissolving back into a fog.

"What can I do?' thought Ovid. "I cannot fulfill this vow. It's turning my mind into so much filth."

But now, in a fit of inspiration, looking down at Alyssa roasting hot dogs, stirring a pot of chili, spitting, farting, acting in all ways as a man ought to, Ovid saw his magnum opus awaiting him in this vision. Racing downstairs, rushing up to

Alyssa at his charcoal grill, Ovid could hardly contain his joy. "That's it! I'm writing a book about a man in a woman's body," said Ovid to his son.

"Oh, God," said Alyssa, cringing. "No, don't. I insist. I don't want you writing about this. It's hard just living it. I don't want it in a book."

"Why not?" said Ovid, looking hurt.

"It's too hard to think about right now," said Alyssa. "I just want out, you know?"

"Out of what?" Ovid said.

"Out of this human incarnation. I wish I was an animal among animals, you know, just a body with no conscious thoughts. A total id," Alyssa said.

"Don't say such things," said Ovid, wanting to say: *A body without conscious thought isn't a total id—it's a total idiot.* Ovid was thinking about Durand Durand's last words, and about all his posturing just prior to that fatal drop. It was harrowing to think that Alyssa was going through a similar quandary as Durand Durand, and as was Ovid, as do all thinking things whom God afflicts with doubt.

"Do you miss Mom?" Alyssa said to Ovid, as Ovid was wrapping his bratwurst in a bun full of raw onions and spicy brown mustard.

"I miss Anna horribly," said Ovid, putting down his brat, "and Aaron, too."

"So why don't you go back to Wisconsin?" Alyssa said.

"I cannot," Ovid said mournfully. "I wish...," but Ovid could not finish making his wish. Starting to sob, Ovid didn't want Alyssa to watch him fall apart. Nothing could stop Ovid from running away.

According to Judaic tradition, King Solomon said, "Find, in my kingdom, a magic ring that, if a happy man looks upon it, will turn sad, and if a sad man looks upon it, will turn happy." Looking high and low for a such a ring, a rabbi finally found a man who took from his sack a ring of gold with this inscription writ upon it: "This too shall pass."

This too shall pass.

Which is to say, if you just can't stand this stupid world and find that you want to opt out of this confining mortality, Richard-Cory-fashion... just wait. And if you think your happy plans will stay happy, and that glorious path in front of you will always point upwards, with no summit past which you will fall... just wait.

In proclaiming it his wish not to submit to an author, Alyssa found a bond with Ovid surpassing blood: of two souls wanting to run away from all authorial scrutiny. Ovid did not want an Author capturing all his motions, his idiosyncratic way of talking, his tics, his faux pas, his poor dialog. Alyssa had run away to avoid a watchful sibling, just as Ovid had run away to avoid his watchful Author.

But Ovid also had an obligation to Durand Durand, that ghost of an autistic romantic OuLiPoan, to uphold his lipogrammatic spirit by writing out his own. And no topic thus far was so inspiring to Ovid as that of Alyssa's plight—a man hiding within a woman's body, facing a world that is not only disapproving of it, but, out of its ignorant shortcomings, cannot grasp it.

Ovid's plan was to cloak his story's origin by shifting its location to Richmond, Virginia, in 1864, during this country's Civil War. Imagining Alyssa as a Virginia-born Joan of Arc, Ovid had his protagonist honor a calling from God to go fight for a Union army, kin against kin, turning martyr for his convictions. Ovid didn't think that Alyssa was actually planning on dying nobly for abolitionism, obviously, but it was this dynamic—of living, fighting, and dying as a man, but still not having a lawful right to cast a ballot for Abraham Lincoln—that was so intriguing to Ovid.

But as good as it sounds, Ovid could not do it. This paralysis had nothing to do with Alyssa, but was all of his own making.

Staring at his pad and clipboard, using an old-fashion quill and an inkstand, Ovid sank into a torpor, waking up at midnight with nothing but confusion to show for it. If Ovid had had a touch of Midas at all, it was lost now. His hands could turn nothing to gold but gold. Soon it was January, and Ovid was hardly starting in with Lincoln's inauguration. His Civil War story had no Civil War in it.

Though his writing was failing by any standard, his bond with his son was as good as any dad could ask for. Ovid and Alyssa took up fishing in bayou country for a day or two, but having run into a situation involving two angry gators, took walks around town now. In Wisconsin, it was snowing, but in Louisiana, it was a warm day, and Ovid and Alyssa took a stroll into Pillowtown.

"This is as bad as Jack Nicholson in Shining. All work and no play is making Ovid a dull boy," said Ovid.

"Who?" said Alyssa, who didn't know film actors as Ovid did.

"C'mon! You don't know Jack Nicholson?" Ovid was using his digits to list all of Jack Nicholson's famous films. "*Shining, Chinatown, Hoffa, Prizzi's Honor, About Schmidt....*" Ovid was having difficulty coming up with a sixth. "*Batman?* Uh... *Mars Attacks?*"

"I saw *Mars Attacks*. It was dumb," said Alyssa.

"That's his point!" Ovid said. "Tim Burton is showing how sci-films today don't maintain that wondrous quality that was such an inspiration for all our old dramas. It's a classic, ironic, iconoclastic film."

"Sorry, I didn't know it was so taboo to say what my opinion is," said Alyssa, dripping with sarcasm.

Ignoring Alyssa, Ovid said, "But it's no *Chinatown*, a classic noir by Roman Polanski, starring Jack Nicholson as a working dick—this guy is straight out of Scotland Yard, basically (and I'm not thinking of Watson)—who is looking into a woman's suspicions about an unfaithful husband, but in doing so, finds out about all kinds of killings. It's a conspiracy plot, but not what you'd think at first. It all winds up—"

"Don't spoil it," said Alyssa, adding sarcastically, "I might watch it."

As Ovid was talking, his arm was around Alyssa's waist, hugging him tightly.

This fond sight, though, did not satisfy Pillowtown's local old-lady population, who saw in this vision only a spill-off from Jazz City's annual Mardi Gras, and thought of Ovid as an urban voluptuary bringing his immoral ways to this small town.

Rumors circulating among this group had it that Ovid was not simply a dad with a bad habit for writing, but a libidinous playboy with a lust for young girls, and now that Ovid was hugging Alyssa in public, what this crowd saw was a lurid old man with his girl-toy. This appraisal of his situation was, obviously, wrong on both accounts (Ovid was not promiscuous, and Alyssa was not a girl).

Soon, a cop car would start patrolling that small span of road that ran in front of Konstantinos' mansion, circling around and around all day long (and doing doughnuts at night). By January thirty-first, a "landscaping" van would park right in front of his building, watching, waiting for Ovid to show up with his "girl-toy" again, gratuitously hugging in public. Ovid was starting to worry that a mob of torch- and pitchfork-carrying old folks was about to run him out of town.

As far as Ovid and Alyssa's ambitions to avoid scrutiny go, this was back-tracking significantly, and on that day Ovid and Alyssa ran away again. Absconding at night, abducting his son again, Ovid took off towards Colorado, with this thought cycling through his brain again and again: "This too shall pass. This too shall pass."

THIRD BOOK

First Part

Officially, nothing is wrong with Ovid—no missing limbs, no old wounds, nothing chronic or viral or fatal. Ovid is just *off*. Abnormal psychologists throughout this world should find a diagnosis for his particular brand of paranoia (or just plain anoia): so far, his condition is not found in any diagnostic manual—to show such strong faith in his Author, but to go against him, to thwart him all along, to abandon his family for unknown lands, just to avoid his watchful ubiquity.

Ovid is an original; you must grant him that. A man unafraid of running away from it all. A prodigal son on vacation. But his simplicity—his ignorant outlook in all things—is astounding. Ovid cannot grasp this obvious fact: His Author is not just a monomaniacal Ahab scouring this world for a giant fish (or, actually, an aquatic mammal), with no rational motivation to inform him; nor a school principal taking disciplinary action on a wayward pupil, for acting up in class; nor a burglar who will gain from his loss, by taking a piddling sum out of his bank account. Ovid is raising his fist *to God.*

Call him Anonymous. A notorious criminal. A ninja assassin. A Roman gladiator with a broadsword. A psycho killing robot or half-human cyborg.

Call him Dracula. Wolfman. Bigfoot. Igor. Quasimodo.

Call him Baudrillard's simulacrum. A post-Lacanian ghost. Call him Author, if you want. Call him anything. As long as you don't call him _____. It is taboo.

Focus on Ovid:

Ovid is driving into Colorado Springs, around Kansas, via Oklahoma, trying to outwit his Author. But his Author can always follow him, always find him. What a pitiful bid to avoid scrutiny by his Author, to throw off his bonds by hopping into a truck and driving, driving, driving! Is this all that a man with an autonomous will can do? If so, it isn't much. Or it's as much of an autonomous will as an ant has, scurrying around on a rug, not knowing that, in an instant, a sadistic kid with a scissors could split him in two at his thorax, or burn him to a crisp with a magnifying glass.

Ovid's Author sits at his laptop and thinks about indulging this whim, of burning Ovid, or cutting him in two. But as long as Ovid is still his protagonist, this is not an option. His only solution is to annoy Ovid in small ways, such as causing his car to run out of gas, only fifty yards from a gas station, so that Ovid has to go out and push his Toyota for a block or two. Or changing highway signs to throw him off track, putting him onto a roundabout, a rotary, always circling, switching back, trying to turn, but failing, flailing, falling short of his goal. Or making road work occur during rush hour, so that traffic sits still for hours, and it is not until morning that Ovid can go on his way again.

This striving of Ovid's—to avoid his Author—is tantamount to apostasy, abandoning a faith in authorship that runs in his Author's blood. It is an insult, an affront to his dignity as a living thing, that a fictional man should try to cast his vision off so casually. Was his Author simply a coat that Ovid had bought on discount at *Macy's*, that you can discard on a whim?

Right now our protagonist is pulling into a gas station, turning off his car, going to pay with a Visa card, using his pump (with his door still ajar), and all throughout, a hobo is watching Ovid (staring, actually), holding up a sign that says, "Will Work for Food," which is such an ordinary sign that Ovid almost looks away, but can't. Fixating on this man's hat (an Abraham Lincoln kind of top-hat), and on his facial hair (an Abraham Lincoln kind of facial hair), Ovid thinks back to his Civil War story, and with his usual paranoia, starts imagining that this man is from OuLiPoCorp, in Colorado Springs with a singular goal: to obtain Ovid's book.

"Stop following us!" Ovid shouts from his gas pump. But Lincoln just grins and turns around his sign, which now says, "Look for Signs All Around You."

Constraints abound. On trucks, on billboard ads, on a walkway, in a parking lot, signs limiting human activity clamor for room, making a cacophony of words, assaulting both sound and sight.

"As soon as you look upon a sign," Ovid thinks, "you know what it says. It hits you subconsciously. And, usually, you follow its instructions."

As Ovid is looking around him frantically, Abraham Lincoln is hobbling toward him, saying, "Boy! Don't play with your food! Don't talk with your mouth full! Stop using your hands! Try using a fork, for crying out loud!"

Walking back to his car, for an instant Ovid thinks, "Which of us is crazy?" Hopping back into his car and starting up his ignition, Ovid says to Alyssa, "It's back to Wisconsin for us."

"What?" says Alyssa, in obvious dismay.

"You and I must go back to Madison, right now," says Ovid, and, although Alyssa can't pick up on it, Ovid is winking at him. "That's right, darling. Ma-di-son." *Wink-wink.*

"But what if I don't want to go back to Madison?" Alyssa says.

Sighing, Ovid says, "OK, *not* Madison, but back to our long and winding road."

"But why? I want to stay, just for tonight. What's so bad about Colorado that you and I can't stay for a night or two?" Alyssa says, showing his colors as a stubborn high school kid.

"Colorado Springs isn't right for us. Too many runaways and vagabonds. Too many cooks can spoil a soup." Ovid couldn't think of anything good to say.

"But I'm not a runaway. I'm with *you*, Dad," says Alyssa.

Switching tactics now, Ovid puts on a frown. "Look. OuLiPoCorp *knows* I'm in Colorado, so I can't hang around. I'm sorry. You can stay, but I'm going," Ovid says.

"Dad, that's so paranoid!"

"No, no," says Ovid, pointing out his window, "Look at that Abraham-Lincoln- looking hobo to our right. That guy is staring at us, no?"

Alyssa looks. "Dad... if that was an amalgam of Abraham Lincoln, Richard Nixon, *and* Bill Clinton—it still shouldn't shock you. This world is full of nut-jobs. And if that man is *actually* Abraham Lincoln, I'd want to stick around and talk to him, wouldn't you?"

Ovid isn't laughing. "OuLiPoCorp wants my book," says Ovid in horror.

"What hubris! What vanity! This is so narcissistic of you. It's all about *you*, isn't it?" Alyssa says, angrily.

"No, it's not that. Look…," but Ovid can't put his words straight. "All right, just tonight. But tomorrow, at 6 a.m. sharp, I *am* going, with or without you."

"OK," Alyssa says, if only to humor him.

Alyssa and Ovid stay up past midnight, talking about flying to Hawaii, possibly, or going down to Patagonia (which was Butch Cassidy's last vacation), or how about driving north to Canada, to Yukon, or Alaska? "Gold-panning," Alyssa says, jokingly.

Ovid laughs, too, and says, apropos of nothing, "Why is it that I always find right-thinking folks in this country saying 'I'll just go to Canada,' if things go badly, usually during an inauguration of a right-wing politician?"

It was January now, and Bush Junior's inauguration, part two, was just days ago—a wound without a scab, oozing blood and pus.

"It probably has to do with avoiding a draft," Alyssa says. "Nobody wants to stick around if you know it's your own blood that will spill. So… go to Canada. Why not?"

Thinking of old W again, Ovid says, "But that's just what any right-wing politician wants: for all conflicting opinions to go away and allow our country—with all its glorious history, its abundant plains and mountains, its industry and productivity—to go straight into *his* hands, with which to conduct a war. *I* say, bring in as many Canadians as you can into *our* country, and with such a radical voting bloc, that status quo buffoon wouldn't carry Florida *or* Ohio."

"Wow," Alyssa says, not unkindly, "I didn't know you had such a political disposition."

"I study history, so I try to maintain a long vision of things, and not form an opinion of any topic too hastily. But this…," Ovid says, growing furious at this thought.

Look at this man, thinking so highly of his own opinions! His linguistic assault on his country's dictator will do nothing to stop an onslaught of a non-industrial Third World country. And it will not stop his Author from committing mass acts of annihilation. It cannot stop his Author crying "Havoc!" and slipping out his own dogs of war.

For Ovid's Author *is* at war with him, though Ovid is not in command of any army, is not a high-ranking official, nor a corporal or major, but a lowly grunt—an insouciant pawn—cannon-bait, and food for worms.

Naturally you know by now who Ovid's Author is, and that I am it, and that Ovid is a victim of a malicious mind busy plotting his undoing.

I am all-knowing, and Ovid will fall into my trap. Ovid is caught. As soon as Ovid took off in his car, abandoning his darling Anna to a living widowhood and his son Aaron to half-orphan status, Ovid was caught. For, though I cannot kill him, I can bring anguish, agonizing his soul by thwarting his passions, taking away all that Ovid is fond of.

Having Ovid run out of gas is not all that I will do to him. As Ovid's Author, I am not just an obnoxious thorn in his foot; I am villainous—a wrathful God wishing harm upon Adam, an Abraham willing to kill his own firstborn son.

Say it, Ovid: "This too shall pass."

Part Two

"Ovid is missing?" I say, sitting at my laptop, staring into my monitor. "How?" Whilst I was talking to you, clarifying things, going on and on about my war with Ovid—on hiatus from narrating his day in all its minutia—our protagonist ran away again, taking his son with him.

But how? I was *watching* Ovid. I had my sights not only on his body, but in his mind, within his brain, monitoring his thoughts.

Was it Alyssa? Could that girl-boy pull off such a stunt, abducting his dad so skillfully on a wintry moonlit night?

I just can't map it out. Supposing Ovid is on a graph, with an X-axis and Y-axis, and four quadrants I'll mark A, B, C, and D (following from A, moving as would hands on a clock—B is in top right position, and C is in bottom right position). How far could Ovid go in just six hours (which is how long I forgot to watch him for)? Not far, I don't think. But I am scanning Colorado with my authorial spotlight, trying to find him, and nothing is showing up. Standing on our right, in a Y-position (Kansas), is my worldly avatar, Paco, looking high and low for him. To our North, Man from Montana is passing through Wyoming, also looking for Ovid. Within Colorado, too, our simulacra of Abraham Lincoln has quit his log cabin in Illinois and is launching a full manhunt. All of us surround him, closing in, but can find nothing, nothing at all.

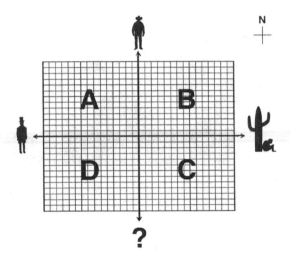

It will not do. Vision is conical, and my scouts can only find that which is in a triangular path of sight from any singular point. And from this vista, from up on high, it's as though Ovid is scurrying around on a Monopoly board—a flat land of cards and chits and plastic buildings, too small for my sight to catch anything. I can control this world, but I cannot go into it. I can only play my hand as good as I can. Buy a railroad. Pick a card. Go to jail. Do not pass Go.

"OK, don't panic," I say. "Ovid is not that sharp." A Harvard boy, I grant you, but only as smart as his transcript. I could catch him without much difficulty, as soon as I finish figuring it out—what is south of Colorado? It's a blot on my map, a lacuna on my graph, a flaw in my algorithm. What am I missing? I want to know!

Ovid is missing. My protagonist! Without him, my story is out of focus, a blur, as if looking through a glass darkly. It fogs up; I cannot go on. I hit a stumbling block—a writing block, you might say, or a road block, just as I had put in Ovid's path as that irritating man was trying to run away.

Now, I must scan this book's margins for a drop of ink or blood—an involuntary spill, which hints at a plan going awry, as Ovid's must. Tracking him down is not difficult, as long as I know what I'm looking for: a trail of alarm and confusion, a frantic spinning around, pivoting on a coin; signs of languor, or a flagging spirit. For Ovid is not truly good at anything but running away. And Ovid can only run for so long. I can always follow him, always find him. As long as I know what I'm looking for.

For now, I fix my spotlight on a Man From Montana, who will invariably cross paths with Ovid. A cowboy hat, worn down to a dull gray color; a pair of cowboy boots with spurs; a stubbly chin, a pinch of chaw in his lip, a pistol at his hip, and a surly way of walking at you, flaring his nostrils and frowning, that brings to mind an angry bull, or as his mood cools off, a *matador* fighting with an angry bull.

Man From Montana is sitting at a dusty bar in Cody, Wyoming—a town that was, prior to this, stomping ground for Bill Cody and Wild Bill Hickok; and prior to that, part of what was known as Lakota country. Man From Montana is sipping a Bud, propping his boots up on a chair, waiting for Ovid to show up at his door. A man who can wait is as good as a bloodhound for tracking down nomads. His ability to stay totally still is what finally brings his victims to him. Ovid may go around this country again and again, constantly, without stopping, but his circumnavigation will only bring him back to this spot, a dodgy old saloon in Cody, Wyoming. And a Man From Montana is waiting.

An orphan (though I think of him as my own son), a product of a tough country upbringing, a mark on his brow, and in his own way a kind of nomad, too, Man From Montana is also known as Cain—Cain, who did a prison stint in Alcatraz for killing a man born of his own blood. And a gold star on his shirt says two things: Cain is a lawman now, and Cain is not afraid to proclaim it.

"So who you in town to catch?" asks a girl, a platinum blond with intoxicating lips—a mouth so luscious it cannot avoid comparison to a fruit, both sugary and sour, and so full of pulp that its skin strains to contain it.

"I'm just having a drink or two," Cain says. "I'm dry is all."

"You must not know our local customs, cowboy," says this girl.

"What? You don't allow guns in your saloon?" Cain says.

"I do. But I was talking about this custom: A lawman out of his jurisdiction has to buy his barmaid a drink," Blondy says, flashing a grin and showing off that mouth.

Cain finds it amusing, but sad, that a girl with such savory lips and a young Dolly-Parton look has to walk across a room to pick up a guy. In old days—Cain's halcyon days of courtship and chivalry—that girl's suitors would stand all in a row, just hoping for a kind word, with no thought of scoring. "I'm on duty," says Cain, "and it ain't right for a gal to ask a man for favors. In a fair world, I'd ask *you* for a favor."

"Huh. I don't know if I just got a turn-down, or a pickup, or what-all," that girl says. "I'm just admiring your gold star and pistol is all. It's so chic, it rings phony." Blondy grins, "You'll fit right in with this crowd."

Cain looks around at a group of bar patrons in cowboy drag, at a man trying to pass off as a squaw, at a stool with wood chipping off of it, and a bar top worn down to look fashionably old.

"Look at this dump," says Blondy "Look at it. It's full of kids playing cowboys and Indians. This cowboy-bar stuff is Hollywood bullshit, don't you think?"

"I don't know. It's got four walls and a roof," Cain says, and shrugs, spitting out a wad of tobacco into a spittoon not far from his arm.

"That's my tip jar," Blondy says with a frown, pointing to a brass pot, now brown with spit.

Cain snorts. "What, nobody spits into that spittoon?"

"That's a first," Blondy says. "Our patrons got what I call 'smoking tobacco' now. You know about it?"

Cain snorts again, and Blondy is thrown off guard by his booming laugh. "I can't stand smoking tobacco," Cain says, pointing at his can of Bud, "In fact, I'm about sick of this stinking air as it is."

"So you ain't no Marlboro man," Blondy says with a shrug. "What's with your scar?" Blondy asks, both as a justification to touch him on his brow and out of actual curiosity.

"It's not a scar; it's my mark of Cain," says Cain.

"What's that, a birthmark?" Blondy asks.

"Sort of…. Look, I don't want you to think I'm standing you up or nothing, but I'm anticipating a visitor soon, so…."

"A gal?" Blondy wants to know.

"A man. I'm on duty, you know."

"Is it a bust?" Blondy asks him, inclining toward him, as if for a kiss, giving him a gratuitous bosom shot through a V of thin, pink fabric.

Cain nods, stoically.

"OK. Go book him, captain," Blondy says with a wink. Walking away from him, Blondy says, "Just so you know, I got handcuffs, if you forgot yours."

For months, Cain shows up of a morning, drinks all day, and stays until closing, always claiming that his visitor is on his way. This bar, Pink Lady Saloon, brings in an unusual amount of foot traffic for such a shantytown pub, and it's full up on Friday and Saturday nights, and Cain is always watching, waiting, for that instant—for Ovid to walk through that door, and sit across from him, as if out of instinct. But it's always almost-him, or not-at-all-him; or it's his old pal Raymond Q, out on a cross-country drinking tour (and who practically forgot who Ovid is). Cain must wait, and sip his drinks slowly.

As it turns out, Blondy isn't a Dolly Parton so much as an Anna Kournikova or Ivana Trump. Blondy was in fact born Ina Ivanovich, a Russian girl from Moscow, brought up in a family of six boys (Boris, Dmitri, Ivan, Fyodor, Vladimir, and Pushkin), this family's only baby girl (whom Boris took to nicknaming "Pumpkin-Butt," for Ina's round form, which would grow at last into a buxom bottom).

On holidays, Ina looks sadly upon Cain, trying to bring him to a family occasion out of pity, but Cain always says no. On All-Hallow's Day (as Ovid would always call it, having grown up in London), Ina brings him a card with a pumpkin on it, and a black cat, and a witch riding on a broom. Ina brings a bag of candy, too, and a cowboy outfit (not that it will do him any good). Around Thanksgiving, Ina brings him a cornucopia full of fruit, and a card showing pilgrims and Indians sharing yams and corn. (Trading food for *alcohol* and *guns* is what it *was*, thinks Cain, indulging his inclination to spoil any Hallmark holiday.)

On Christmas Day, though, Cain cannot say no. For Ina puts on a Santa Claus outfit, trudging through blinding snow and roaring wind just to bring him a stack of gifts. "What a girl," Cain can't stop thinking, "What a girl, going through such trials just to bring joy to this cowboy's Christmas."

But, far from having a family Christmas, as Ina was originally planning, Cain and Ina find a spot away from all of that hum and murmur from Pink Lady Saloon's daily travails. Camping out in a snowy plain, still chilly from that morning's frost, Ina and Cain sit among stars and sing camping songs until moondown.

"So what's up in Montana, anyway?" Ina says, snuggling into a down quilt.

"Lots of things," Man From Montana says.

"Big Sky country?"

"Yup."

"Do you actually call it that?"

Cain nods. "It is what it is."

Cain adds a log to his growing stack of burning wood. Huddling downwind from its blazing warmth, with a woman's body lying against his, Cain allows his mood to calm, his guard to drop.

"So who's so grand that you would wait around all day, Monday through Sunday, month upon month, just to catch him? Is it a criminal?"

"Nah, it's just Ovid," says Cain, without going into it.

Tangling up in a Christmas quilt, this dyad—a pair of loving fools, groping and moaning in a knot of limbs—lift and fall on this snowy ground until night spills into morning.

How romantic.

But as morning dawns, and Cain puts on his pants, pulls a shirt on, and stands facing a mound of cold, burnt wood, it occurs to him that, if Ovid *did* stop by Pink Lady Saloon on that day, Cain would miss him, and not only Ovid, but Cain, too, could fall out of favor with his Author.

Third Part

Anna is drying laundry, laying it out on an old-fashion drying rack, using Ovid's lint-brush, ironing his button-down shirts as though anticipating Ovid will walk through that front door in an hour or so—waiting for him, as Cain is waiting for him, as I am waiting for him. As all of us must await Ovid.

I am watching Anna, though I know that Ovid is not going to walk in that door. Ovid wants to rub it in—that his plan is working—to vanish from my sight, as if in a cloak of invisibility. Throughout this vanishing act, Ovid paid no thought to Anna.

Ovid has happily quit his darling Anna for a living widow-hood, in pursuit of an imaginary Atlantis. (That is what I am insinuating into Anna's brain, anyway, as Anna folds his socks and hangs up his corduroy pants.)

Anna quits drying laundry to sit down and watch TV. And I watch Anna watching TV. And, in a way, Ovid's TV is also watching us.

As Anna is watching TV, Anna is also murmuring softly, as though to Alyssa, "Don't worry, baby, it's OK. Ovid will bring you back to Mama. Don't worry, baby, it's OK. Ovid will bring you back to Mama." Though it is not Alyssa, but I, who sits with Anna, sharing a couch with Anna, though Anna has no way of knowing it. I am watching Anna now, as long as Ovid is away.

It is so good, not to inhabit a physical body—to simply watch, to float inconspicuously through this world. I know why Ovid wants to author his own book, and to avoid scrutiny from *his* Author. It is a triumph of will, a summit of all human ambition, to turn into God's first man, Adam, naming all his animals; or, most ambitious of all, to turn into God, making Adam out of clay.

An ad for Absolut Vodka is on TV. It's my fault. I put it on. (I had to. A TV spot for hard liquor is an unusual sight on a Monday night.) It is an ad, I might add, that is also unusu-ally convincing. Anna is blown away by this sight—a young man with a strong chin, a six-foot arm span, a tight butt, and a broad back, dousing his muscular body with Absolut Vodka. Anna is thirsty.

How long can Anna wait for Ovid? Shouldn't a man who abandons a woman know that a woman will not wait too long for him? "I should *do* things," Anna thinks. "But what? What can I do all on my own, without my husband?"

It may sound plain to you, but it is not so obvious for a woman such as Anna, who has grown so familiar with lint and laundry and missing socks, to know how to go about having fun without a husband in tow. As far back as Anna could think of, "fun" had always brought pain. First, you would go out for a round of drinks, and in not too long you'd sink into a torpor, liquoring up, without stopping, for months. In fact, at a particularly low point, this family woman had fought with an addiction that put Anna's body into a virtual coma.

"Damn it. I'll go drinking," Anna thinks, still watching that surprisingly long vodka ad. "It's not so hard to join that club. Now that I'm on my own, I could drink all night if I want to. As long as I don't wind up in Alcoholics Anonymous tomorrow."

This vodka ad is going on and on and on. In fact, it lasts all throughout this flashback, in which Anna is shown to harbor a sordid history as an alcoholic. As Anna walks away from this TV, going out to a bar, this young TV actor lights a match, igniting his body from crown to foot, which is soaking in alcohol. In TV-land, his body slowly burns down to nothing. (I put that touch in for dramatic pomp—for symbolism, you could say.)

Anna finds a smoky bar with dim lights and no windows. It's a working-class bar, not a frou-frou Madison hippy bar. All of its patrons watch football on TV.

"So, what's your poison?" a barman asks, with tattoos all along his arms.

"What's on tap?" Anna wants to know.

"Sam Adams, Rolling Rock, Pabst. But if I was you, I'd go for our vodka," Tattoo-guy says, holding it up for show. "It's Absolut."

Anna looks at him aslant. "It looks as though this world is conspiring to ply my gut with vodka. But you know what I say? 'Just say no.'"

Anna's barman winks. "You can't say no to unavoidability."

Anna turns this thought around for a bit. Though I can control Anna's mind, I want Anna to sink into a psychological stupor without my prompting it. So, for an instant, I allow Anna to think.

"No vodka. How about a gin and tonic?"

"Coming right up," Barman says.

Though I was watching Anna's thoughts with my Authorial sight, it wasn't my guiding hand that got Anna drunk that night. It was wholly Anna's doing. Not all things that occur in this world do so on my whim. Ovid is proof of that. Mostly, I stand back and watch, and it all unfolds of its own accord, and I simply laugh at all this human folly—this slapstick and hijinks. It's my only sport (I don't watch football on TV, as do this midnight crowd of hoi polloi).

As a drunk woman in a bar, Anna is hit on, naturally. But no amount of drink can turn Anna unfaithful. On a downward spiral, on a wayward path, Anna is still a far cry from Ina (and Ina's cowboy liaison), caught in an illicit tryst. By constitution a monogamous woman, Anna is not out for a night of hanky-panky, but in pursuit of distraction only. Though Anna is not about to go skydiving, as Ovid did.

Anna stays until closing, upon which hour, stumbling out onto Myrmidon Road, Anna waits for a bus, and hops on, to locations unknown.

Having spun round and around Madison for an hour or two, Anna finally pays a visit to Konstantinos, and, knocking on his door, finds it slightly ajar.

Looking into his living room, and spotting nobody within it, Anna walks right in. Not surprisingly, a flask of vodka is standing upright on his ottoman.

"OK," Anna says aloud, to nobody in particular. "OK, OK, I'll drink vodka, if you want!"

Anna quickly downs a shot, swallowing it all in a big hungry gulp. Soon Anna is sipping straight out of Konstantinos' flask. By midnight, Anna has drunk up all his vodka supply.

Drunk as a skunk now, Anna is thinking, "Why don't I go skinny-dipping in Konstantinos' backyard pool? Nobody is around." Anna strips down and walks out back to his pool.

As it turns out, Anzora is swimming in Konstantinos' pool—which, naturally, is also Anzora's pool. As it turns out, Anzora was up all night drinking, too, and was not anticipating company—was in fact having a night of sinful privacy. But Anzora puts on a happy mug for Anna. Anzora pulls Anna in for a big Diamantaras hug (both without bathing suits on), and brings Anna down to a lit patio. Two nudists walking down a stairway.

"It's so good of you to pop in," Anzora says to Anna, smilingly, ignoring Anna's vacant-looking pupils.

"Uh-huh," Anna says, still in shock at running into Anzora.

"So what did you do all night?" Anzora asks, curious to know how drunk Anna is, and what Anna is up to at 2 a.m.

"You know, I was out and about, doing this and that," says Anna, hazily, but Anzora thinks Anna is just acting coy.

"Hmmm... is that so?" Anzora must find it all so amusing. "And what about you-know-who?"

"I just pray that Alyssa is still living," says Anna, caught in a half-truth (Anna wants Alyssa back, and without harm, but praying has nothing to do with it).

"I know how to find out if Alyssa is still living," says Anzora. "Do you know how to contact spirits?"

"I don't think so," Anna says, thinking for a flash that Anzora is talking about "spirits" as in alcohol.

"*I* can contact spirits, using a Ouija board!" Anzora pulls out a board with various symbols on it, mostly familiar, but much of it oddly cryptic-looking, too. It's an occult toy. Mystical kitsch. How could it actually work? But Anna is willing to try anything at this point, if only to ward off oncoming doldrums.

So Anna and Anzora sit down without talking, allowing a mood of calm to fall upon this yard. Background music pours out from a radio. Subtly rippling, Anzora's pool throws off a turquoisy light. All is still, and not still. All is in motion, but paradoxically static, as Anna and Anzora sit down with a

Ouija board, communing with spirits that may or may not actually swarm about.

"What do I do?" Anna asks.

"Just don't think," says Anzora, as though it isn't a difficult thing to do, to stop thinking on command.

But, possibly on account of drinking four gin and tonics and a flask of vodka, Anna has no difficulty zoning out, and giving total hand-control to any abiding spirits that might inhabit this suburban backyard patio.

What an opportunity for an Author to work his magic! It's as though Anna and Anzora *know* how much fun it is to mold unconscious minds, to control individual actions, to play with living dolls. I only wish my playthings could know my handiwork for what it is— that it is *I*, guiding it all.

Palms down, two pairs of hands start to shift this plastic disk around a board. Drifting now on its own accord (it looks that way to Anna and Anzora, anyway), this flat, triangular disk darts around from symbol to symbol, until it forms a full word. Two full words, in fact. But I cannot stop my guiding hand from touching a vacant spot first, though I do not know what it could signify.

Finally, it forms two words: *Pluribus Unum.*

"Pluribus? What is a Pluribus?" Anna asks. "Is it a school bus? Or an omnibus?"

"Pluribus Unum...." Anzora thinks out loud. "It's Latin."

"But do you know any Latin?" asks Anna.

"No, but my son was taught this in high school not long ago. 'Out of many....'" Anzora stops short, trying to think of what follows. "Out of many, *what*? 'Out of many' isn't a full thought. What follows 'Out of many...'?"

"It's our national motto," Anna says. "It's on all our coins, and on all our dollar bills, too. But I don't know its full form." It's a conundrum. I can't work it out, just as Anna and Anzora cannot work it out. Part of it is missing. But I don't know which part. Pluribus Unum! Pluribus Unum! What is missing? I was hoping Anna could clarify it for us, but alas, this girl of Ovid's is no good—not to him, not to his Author, and most of all not to Anzora (who, you must know by now, was truly out swimming at midnight on account of having just slain an unfaithful husband).

Anzora was just finishing drowning Konstantinos in his own pool, as Anna was brought into this situation. Noticing Anna was totally drunk, Anzora said nothing, using Ouija as a tool of distraction. But now, as Anzora thought about it, Anna was a liability—a wild card, who could only spoil it for Anzora.

"What's that in your pool?" Anna says, noticing a big blur floating on its top.

"I don't know. Why don't you go find out? I'm just drying off, so I'm gonna go and find a drying rag. You can stay out for as long as you want and swim." Anzora stood up and took a walk down to find Konstantinos' handgun.

Go for a swim, Anna. It's a parting gift, from your Author. Dip your foot in, first. Try splashing a bit on your arms. Spring up and down on its diving board. But don't hang back too long. Jump right in. It's warm. Trust your Author. Don't wait up for Ovid.

Part Four

So much backstabbing, I almost want to put a stop to it all. It's sick, and unnatural, all this conspiracy and dissimulation. A man having an affair. A woman killing a man for having an affair. A woman killing a woman for finding out that this first woman had slain a man for having an affair. This moral corruption, it just turns on—I don't know why, or how—and sustains, gains gravity, finds low ground, bottoming out.

Not that Konstantinos' actions didn't warrant it. Contrarily, Konstantinos had it coming to him. I was glad to watch him go. But Anna! Anna was Ovid's sanctuary, his rock, his only moral normality. Without Anna, Ovid is nothing but a crazy loon circling on a map, hiding from his Author, on a long road to nothing but his own doom. But it's his own fault, right? Ovid brought it on, by trying to run away from it all. And now Anna is unconscious, numb to all human passion and curiosity—corpsy—and starting to go stiff with rigor mortis as I am writing this.

Naturally, it was by my coordination that Anna's fatality was wrought, but it was not *I* who shot off a gun. It was not *I* who sank Anna's body into solid ground. That was Anzora's doing. I was fond of Anna, actually. But sadly, Ovid was not around to guard his most darling inamorata. So it was within all bounds of logic to kill Anna off, as I did, by fiat.

So, is it foul play? Or fair play? Who can say? What do you think? (Did I just ask that? Pay it no mind. It is *my* world. If I want your opinion, I'll ask for it.)

Don't worry about Anna. That is all past now. I won't go back and modify history.

But what will Ovid do now? What will this impractical utopian do without a stabilizing constraint? Our own Quixotic Don has lost his Sancho Panza—his only practical half.

I had thought that Cain might pick up that duty. I had originally sought a run-in 'twixt this Man From Montana and that Man of La Mancha. I was imagining a book full of broad humor and witty *sanchismos*. Aragon and Castilla at war. Old notions of chivalry coupling with today's cynical world. A panoply of pomp and circumstantial irony. An important book. Not a pop-cultural trick book.

This story—of Ovid's flight into a lofty kingdom of authorship, and his gradual fall into his own dirt-born crudity—must do for now. Or, lacking a protagonist, I must ad lib with a man-hunting cowboy waiting for Ovid in a bar in Wyoming.

Cain is again waiting for Ovid (and awaiting his damnation, too, for shirking his duty to his Author). How could Cain do such a thing? It's so disappointing, for a plan to fail so thoroughly, simply on account of a cowboy's inability to contain his libido. What a naughty boy Cain is. What a bad son.

For Ovid *did* show up at Pink Lady Saloon with Alyssa that night (in that instant, as Ovid was caught walking into Pink Lady Saloon's door, Ina was having a blazing orgasm—which may go a long way towards illustrating why Ina would fall so hard for Cain so quickly). *And*, in light of Ina's truancy, Alyssa took on Ina's job as a barmaid. Ina hadn't shown up for work all day, and Ina's boss had no option but to find a barmaid who could work a four-hour shift right away. So, just at that point, Alyssa and Ovid walk in, and voilà!

This is my kind of bar, Alyssa had said to him, looking around at this bar's patrons in drag. *I could work in this bar as long as you want.* Imagining working in this bar, Alyssa thinks up a possibility that did not occur to him at any point in his past: autonomy. Alyssa did savor this possibility: of announcing to Ovid that Wyoming is his final stop. It's no good to run away from your bliss.

But Ovid cut that thought short. Prior to Cain's arrival at Pink Lady Saloon that following morning, Ovid took his things and took flight again, abandoning his own son in a gay cowboy bar in Cody, Wyoming.

Nowadays, Alyssa is working night shift, making a bit of dough off of tips, but not much. And Ovid is still missing. I *would* simply stand back, bystanding, admiring its irony, if it wasn't such a bad turn of luck. I'd laugh out loud if it wasn't causing such pain.

First, Ovid abandons Anna and Aaron in Wisconsin. Now, Ovid abandons Alyssa in Wyoming. What kind of protagonist is this? Ovid is a bad daddy, without a doubt. A total nutjob. Cuckoo.

That's a good thought! I'll put that thought into Cain's mind, so that Cain can pass on this communication to Alyssa.

Look:

"So your old man just up and took off?" Cain says, sitting across from Alyssa (his barmaid) as Ina looks in longingly from a window.

"Yup," says Alyssa, thinking, all throughout this back and forth, that Cain is actually a woman in a man's clothing.

"Now that's just wrong," says Cain, shaking his noggin. "Just plain wrong. It's crazy, is what it is."

"No, it's OK," says Alyssa. "Ovid wants to finish his book, and I'm a distraction."

"You? A distraction? I don't think so," Cain says.

Smiling now, Alyssa says, "That's charming. Thank you."

Cain winks, turning his charm on full-blast. "But now that I think about it, you probably *could* distract a man."

"That's kind of you, but I *am* a man, actually, and I'm not looking for that anyway. I'm looking for a woman… a woman similar to you, in fact."

"A cowgirl?" Cain says with a grin. "You won't find any cowgirls in this dump."

Alyssa looks at Cain aslant. "Won't I?"

"No," Cain says.

"OK," Alyssa says, with a wink. "If you say so."

During this discussion, Ina's fury is growing. Ina has lost a job, a man, and now, all modicum of dignity, too, as this busty Russian barmaid is ogling Cain and Alyssa through Pink Lady Saloon's south window, watching for any sign of flirtation. It's as bad as any country song. Boy finds girl. Boy fucks girl. Boy finds girl two. Boy fucks girl two. And so on and so on.

(I am sorry that I must work with bathroom-wall illustrations. But that is how I was taught to woo a woman, so I thought it might assist you in visualizing that which Ina is imagining with Cain and Alyssa.)

Ina storms in on Cain and Alyssa, pounding a fist down on a bartop in front of Cain. "What's going on, huh, cowboy? What do you plan on doing with this young barmaid?" asks Ina, scowling at Cain. "You two gonna buy a room now, is that it?"

"I'm just chatting, that's all. Anything wrong with it?" Cain says.

"Chatting it up with a sub-par barmaid," says Ina, looking Alyssa up and down. "You slut."

"Um... Can I talk?" says Alyssa. "First of all, I'm not a barmaid. I'm a man, so I'm a barman, actually."

Ignoring Alyssa, Ina says, "How old is that girl, anyway?"

"Young. So? What about you?" says Cain.

"I'm *thirty-two*," says Ina.

Alyssa puts in, "I'm only half as old as you, as of today—" and turning to Cain, adds, "It's my birthday."

"Oh, happy birthday," Cain says to Alyssa. Turning to Ina, Cain says, "How about that? Half as old as you. That ain't so young."

"That's too young," says Ina. "It's against Wyoming's sodomy laws. I don't know how Montanans do things, but in Wyoming—"

"Wait, who said anything about sodomy?" Cain asks.

With an appraising look at Alyssa, Ina says, "It says it's a man."

Cain and Ina both look at Alyssa, trying to find any sign of a man within this woman (a man is hiding within Alyssa, but is hiding so skillfully that Cain and Ina cannot find him).

"Um... I'm not *surgically* a man, if that's what you want to know," Alyssa admits.

"OK," says Cain, to whom Alyssa's words brought about obvious satisfaction.

Ina says, "Man or woman, it's still too young for you. It's statutory."

"Don't talk about laws as though you know. *I'm* a lawman." Cain shows off his gold star.

"Not in this town," says Ina. "It's out of your jurisdiction."

"But wasn't it *you* who said that a lawman out of his jurisdiction has to buy his barmaid a drink?" Cain says, with a smirk.

Alyssa cuts in again with, "Uh... hi, I'm not a barmaid."

Finally, Ina storms off, crying into a napkin. A splotch of ruby lipstick. A drip of mascara. A dab of blush. Ina's napkin is now a colorful swirl of mixing-paint. As Ina shuts Pink Lady Saloon's door, and stands outdoors in a flurry of snow, lit by a lamp with a dying sixty-watt bulb, Ina broods on how to win back Cain's trust, and how to turn this Alyssa situation into Ina's favor. But standing out on a snowy night without a coat on, Ina can't think of anything but Cain's cold pistol.

Cain picks up a toothpick and sighs.

"You should say 'I'm sorry' for what you just did," Alyssa says to him.

"For what now?" Cain says, looking up from his drink.

"To start with, how about for making your woman sad?" Alyssa says. "That's no way for a cowboy to act."

"It's too bad, I'll grant you, but that ain't my doing," Cain says, fatalistically. "Ina is sad of Ina's own volition. And I don't go around apologizing. Not for things I didn't do."

"OK," says Alyssa, standing up. "*I'll* go say 'I'm sorry' *for* you. You just stay put and act proud all night."

"Wait," says Cain. "I want to talk to you, girl."

"Go fuck a goat, cowboy," Alyssa says, and walks out. Cain sits on his own now, shifting in his stool, thinking about what all could go wrong tomorrow.

Ina is sitting down outdoors, crying into both hands. Your ordinary bar patron might think Ina a vagrant, with a dissolving mask of mascara, a dirty napkin, and no coat on.

"Ina..." Alyssa says, "I don't know why you would allow

such a phony to stomp on your loyalty that way."

Ina looks up at Alyssa, saying, "I don't know…. Cain's not so bad, if you know him."

"Sorry," Alyssa says. "Cain hurt you, and hurting you *is* bad."

"You didn't mind his company just now," Ina says. "You two got along as kindly as two pups at a public park."

"It was just a dog-and-pony show. All Cain could talk about is my dad," says Alyssa.

"Who is your dad?" Ina asks.

"Oh, just Ovid," says Alyssa, and Ina smirks knowingly. A plan is just taking form in Ina's conniving brain.

"All guys try and lay it on so thick, but it's always a mask for what guys actually want…." Pausing to draw it out, Alyssa is trying hard to sound worldly and all-knowing, cynical and profound. "Which is just a warm body."

"Nothing wrong with a warm body," Ina says, in a low murmur. Smiling in a matronly way, Ina adds, "Look. I don't want you caught up in all this drama. I can think of a lot of things on a par with a bit of romantic pain. I'm a victim of Cupid's arrow, I know, but it ain't my first trip around."

Alyssa looks lovingly at Ina's stunning lips as Ina talks. "You a cowgirl?"

Ina grins and asks Alyssa to sit down. Just now, Ina is hatching a plan to win Cain back. Knowing that Alyssa is Ovid's child, and that Cain wants to catch Ovid, Ina starts to think how to sway Alyssa into giving him up, asking, "Alyssa, do you know what got into your dad—why Ovid just took off so abruptly?"

"Oh no, not you, too," says Alyssa, kidding with Ina, not knowing what Ina's actual motivation was. "Actually, I don't know. Ovid forgot his journal, though, so it's not too difficult to find out. I can go look, if you want to know so badly."

"A journal? Is that so?" Ina says, finding in Alyssa's admission an opportunity to curry favor with Cain, to win him back. "Is it on you now?"

"No," says Alyssa, "but it's just out back, in my car… which is also my lodgings for now." Alyssa was living out of Ovid's old Toyota.

"You poor thing. Why don't you stay in my flat tonight?" Ina stands up and puts on an anxious look.

"OK," Alyssa says, a tad too avidly. "Just until Habitat for Humanity drops by to build my habitat."

At this point, I must fast-forward to that journal's initial display, as Alyssa unfolds it on his lap. For I too am anxious, avid to spy on Ovid's writing, which contains an obscurity that I cannot account for. I cannot look into Ovid's book without a fictional man or woman as a proxy.

Ina is picking it up now, handling it as though it might turn to dust.

It's a scrapbook of sorts, full of song lyrics, photographs, pay stubs, bric-a-brac, curios. But as Ina flips through it, and I am looking on, Alyssa puts his hand on top of it, closing it off, obscuring it again from my sight. Alyssa holds Ina's hand in his, looks at Ina promisingly, full of conflict, full of sorrow and lust.

"You can't...," Ina says, with a sad-clown frown. "Your mind is old, I know, but your body is still young."

"Don't say that," says Alyssa, stroking Ina's hair. "I want this."

"I want it, too," says Ina. "But not now. It's too soon. I just had my soul torn apart by Cain.... I'm sorry. I'm waxing dramatic again."

"It's OK," Alyssa says, stroking Ina's chin. "I can wait. I know that Cupid will shoot off his arrow again."

"I want to ask you a favor," says Ina cautiously.

"OK. Shoot."

"Would you... is it too much to ask, for you to loan out this journal, for a day or two?" Ina says, bashful now.

"OK," says Alyssa. OK, OK, OK, Alyssa says. What a quick submission! How could Alyssa, a longstanding nonconformist, turn into such a doormat? Naturally, I am glad that Alyssa is giving up Ovid's journal, but it is surprising to find that Alyssa is giving up his dignity, too.

Though just looking at Ovid and Anna is proof that attraction is mystical, unknown to all, including its attractor.

Again and again, I find that, if I want to know what is going on, I must simply sit back and watch. How all my world's inhabitants pray for my support, thinking I am God! But I will not just butt in on a whim, intruding upon an ongoing drama. If my world has a god at all, it is this: a wristwatch wound on its own long ago, putting into a motion a grand plan, in which a microcosm full of clockwork orangutans—chimps without hair—go around acting important, as though born to a lofty function.

It's tiring, coordinating this production, staging this comic play in six acts. I want to know how it all turns out. I will fast-forward to its final paragraph:

Ovid will fall. You will fall, too. As will I. Falling into an abyss, as if shot out of a pod into nothing. An infinity of black, split up by an occasional flash of light, a drifting galaxy, a sun about to nova, a rock floating in slow motion, quasars, stardust. Ziggy Stardust. A starman. A spatial oddity. A grain of sand in orbit. *Ground Control to Major Tom...? Ground Control to Major Tom...?* Gravity pulls on us; and you, I, and Ovid, must follow it, not knowing what awful or amazing thing awaits us.

I want to look into Ovid's journal. Now. I want to not wait. Why is such a straightforward thing so difficult to do? I can control this cosmos. I can undo worlds.

I can fast-forward to its final paragraph. But what I *want* is to know how Ovid could slip past my radar and author his own book. Why must I wait?

Fifth Part

Cut to Aaron: an orphan now, but still basically a boy in high school, carrying on as usual. Frontal shot: Aaron looks distraught, out of sorts—a high school kid who has just found out that his mom is missing (along with his dad and twin sibling, too).

Narrow in on his sad-sack mug: Furrowing his brow, Aaron shows signs of fading, about to nod off. Pan out: a writing class on a Monday morning, his first class today, and as a ring sounds from a hallway, a mob of kids is filing out. An instructor with a prim ponytail and stubbly chin-hair holds Aaron back, to talk with him.

"Thanks for coming to class today," says Mr. Math, Aaron's writing instructor, shuffling away a stack of books, making room for his sad-looking pupil. "I didn't know if you'd show up."

"OK," says Aaron, sitting uncomfortably in his chair. "So what do you want to talk about?"

"I want to discuss your composition for this class, "Null and Void," which isn't actually a composition at all, but a fictional story. I'm just curious, that's all...," Mr. Math says, trailing off.

"What do you want to know?" Aaron says, shyly.

"How do *you* think I should go about grading this composition?" Mr. Math says, handing back Aaron's writing portfolio, which was a story similar to *Lolita* (which book Alyssa had put on his pillow that day of that Alyssa and Ovid ran away), but with a boy, not a girl, as its protagonist. "Should I mark it as an A, B, C, D, or F?"

Aaron shrugs. "That's up to you, sir."

"My point is, Aaron, that you won't fulfill this writing task by writing a silly story about an imaginary family," Mr. Math says, with a stiff nod.

"Oh," says Aaron, thinking it was just a mix-up. "It isn't imaginary. This is my family."

"Ah, but your family *is* imaginary," says Mr. Math, coldly, and Aaron shrinks back. This instructor, Harry Math, knows that Aaron's family is missing, but is capitalizing on this opportunity in a bid to draw Aaron into his Christian camp for young boys. Concocting this story, Mr. Math is praying (and I want you to think about this word's homonym, too) that Aaron, in his mourning, will turn towards God.

Harry Math, as you know, was in a writing class with Ovid long ago, and as much as Harry would try in his Harvard days to bring Ovid into his flock, Harry could not draft him into his quasi-spiritual ways. First, Harry brought a painting of Christ with him to school and put it on a wall in his study. Failing to turn Ovid into a holy man in this way, Harry bought Ovid a book of biblical quotations, with an autograph from its author (not from its original author, obviously), which Harry found in his trash can that night. Trying out a frontal approach, Harry would start inviting Ovid to church on Sundays. But Ovid always said no. Harry's last assault upon Ovid's soul took this form: walking into Ovid's dorm and saying, "Ovid, if you do not turn to God now, I will wind up taking your firstborn son away."

Naturally, Ovid thought Harry was joking, having a bit of fun with Ovid, Harvard's most young prodigy. But Harry did in fact stick to his plan. So now, Harry is moving on to Aaron, who is as young as Ovid was back at Harvard, still forming notions about how his world works.

"Did you run into your family this morning on your way to school? Did your Mom walk you to your bus?" Harry says, as though such a thing could stand as proof. "Do you usually find your dad waiting for you as you go out from school? I don't think that you do."

Aaron looks up, down, and around, as if his classroom is turning and spinning and turning and spinning and turning.

"Wait," says Aaron, holding his arms up, as if to ward off an assault. "Mom said that Ovid was down South, visiting family, and Alyssa, too."

"No," says Harry, with gravity, "I don't think so. You say that this 'Ovid' is down South, and 'Alyssa' too. What about your 'mom'? Is your 'mom' also down South?"

Aaron is almost crying, wanting to say anything at all, but struck dumb by this possibility—that all his childhood was a product of his own imagination: a brutal fiction, with no factual actuality.

"Aaron," says Mr. Math, sounding firm. "I'm going to pass along this book to you, which I think of as a sort of 'manual for living.'" Mr. Math hands Aaron a book upon which is this inscription: *If You Want It, It's Probably Bad for You.* And its author had kindly thought of subtitling it, "A Handbook for Today's Puritan."

So Aaron submits to Christian camp for four months, in an old military barracks up North in Oshkosh, Wisconsin. Day in and day out, his surroundings, his company, his books, his background music—all instruct him how to act worshipful, conspiring to turn Aaron into a Christian automaton, a robot in God's army. During morning "group-talks," Aaron is told by a man in a jogging outfit that God picks only his most faithful for a tour of duty in his kingdom. At first, Aaron is noncompliant, lighting up a match and blowing it out, again and again, in midst of this public oratory, saying "Why is this guy haranguing us?" to his only buddy Carl (who was, prior to Christian camp, a Rastafarian with a chronic smoking habit, and also a nonconformist).

But soon, with a good amount of brainwashing, Aaron starts to buy into this fantasy, that Aaron is not a boy who lost his family, but actually a boy who had no family to start with: no anxious Mom, no oblivious Dad, no oddball twin. Just an orphan kid with a highly idiosyncratic imagination.

Now, post-Christian-camp, post-transformation, post-programming (Aaron's Mind 2.0), Aaron thinks of his situation in an out-of-body sort of way: "I am a boy with no mom or dad—born from nothing." A virgin birth! A son of God! Holy light falls upon him! A crucifix, a stigmata, and a crown of thorns—a Passion of Christ in his own right.

Do not laugh at this hypocrisy. For it is our most truthful plot twist so far. Painfully so. As I am writing this, millions upon millions of individuals in our world go around thinking God is within us (Ha! How would God fit within us, with all of our blood and guts and organs stuffing us full?), and not high up in a cloud, watching, as I am.

As any good son-of-a-God would, Aaron thinks now and again of sacrificing his body for man's sins, and having his spirit float off into his bosom (though, as God, having Aaron in my bosom would carry with it a mystifying paradox). Aaron soon finds, though, that no opportunity for martyrdom pops up. You can't just casually go around asking if humankind wants a third coming of Christ. (According to Aaron's church, Christ's last visit was in May 2002, on a Saturday night. Christ took on physical form, just for an hour or so, until midnight, drinking scotch and sodas at a bar with his cohorts, whom, frankly, Christ found too star-struck and sycophantic for his liking.) But Christ's *third* coming, according to his church, was going to surpass all past visitations, and would bring about this world's final days. So now Aaron has a scatological notion ("a scatological" notion sounds right, anyway—this word, too, probably has a significant homonym) about a rapturous conclusion to this world of sin and sorrow.

But what is most convincing to Aaron is not this apocalyptic vision, nor all this panic about damnation. It is that Aaron is now a fan of Christian rock. According to Aaron, Christian rock has all of hard rock's oomph, with an additional quality that is as surprising and comforting as a bonus track on a Nirvana CD: bliss. For all of hard rock's many charms, Aaron thinks, it is lacking in this: that Christian rock stars stand up and shout out in joy and jubilation, but hard rock stars go on and on complaining about having "no satisfaction." (But today, by contrast, I savor dissatisfaction, draw joy from it, knowing how chronically unhappy all of humankind truly is. This happy Christian stuff just brings about confusion, in my opinion.)

Taking drugs is a must among both kinds of rock music fan. Though, prior to Christianization, Aaron was smoking marijuana primarily, and dropping acid occasionally. Now Aaron is taking Prozac: a happy-making drug, a placid Christian drug, a drug that has FDA approval and is sold at his local pharmacy.

But is Aaron happy? Is a man who is smiling all day and following "God's will" truly happy? Or is "happy" only his domain who follows his id? I don't know. Happy is just a word.

But I do know what a joy it is to Play God, to act out this fantasy in a world that I control, inflicting my wrath upon all who would contradict my chain of command. Such as Ovid, who shuns his Author. Such as Cain, who bucks his duty. Such as Konstantinos, who was just a fly in my soup. And poor Anna, a casualty of war, who simply got in our way.

It is March, and Spring's first thaw hits Wisconsin this month (if you don't know, Oshkosh, is way, way up North—a cold and windy city full of snow). By March, Aaron is a product of thorough conditioning. A sunny disposition, with no inclination toward "doom and gloom," as Mr. Math would put it, Aaron will now flash a quick grin and two thumbs up to all good Christians who cross his path. His clothing is crisp and straight, not grungy or gothic, and his hair is so smooth that it is practically rainproof.

But now, with no clothing on at all, Aaron is washing his hair with shampoo, scrubbing his body with soap, coating his skin with thick, foamy suds. It is a purifying ritual. But, far from Canaan, Aaron is standing in a Jacuzzi in Oshkosh, Wisconsin, about to join God's ranks. Thinking Aaron should probably wash and brush prior to purifying his soul, Ovid's son is taking a bath *and* a baptism.

Finally, a man dunks Aaron into a bathtub. And with this act, Aaron turns into a full Puritan.

You thought I was going to kill him? No, no, no. What do you think I am, a villain? I don't kill kids, including fictional kids. A minor, such as Aaron, is strictly off limits—not at all privy to our chopping block. I might play rough now and again, but it is all in good fun.

Turning Aaron into a Puritan is just as bad; it is tantamount to castrating Ovid's only son (or, his only anatomical son). With no id, Aaron is just a product of social conditioning, and not a man at all.

Ovid, by contrast, is an author who kills kids—his first non-book about Dirty Dick contains an awful protagonist—a failing magician—who cuts a kid in half, but cannot put him back into his original form. A sort of "Humpty Dumpty" motif, you might say. You will not find such mutilations within this book. Only, occasionally, mutilation-by-analogy.

Part Six

This too shall pass.

King Solomon also said, "Cut that baby in half."

A baby boy: A living child. Two young moms: a woman in mourning, and a woman with a son. Both claim rightful status to guardianship of this still-living child. How can you know which baby is which? And how can you know which is that living child's actual mom?

"Cut that baby in half," said King Solomon. "And split it up amongst you."

(

Ovid's is not a happy, triumphant story. Ovid's story is morbid—and not just in a distant post-apocalyptic world, but now. His loss in this war, and his total annihilation, is unavoidably nigh. I ordain it. You might say that Ovid is a visionary. You might say that Ovid is a child prodigy, grown old and sad. But what you won't say—I know for a fact—is that Ovid is a survivor. You know, as much as I do, that Ovid is not long for this world.

If I find Ovid, I will drag his body around Troy on a chariot, circling that city again and again. It is not a victory until Ovid's body is muddy and bloody, his limbs hanging off of his torso as dangling fruit about to fall from a branch.

What famous warrior from *Iliad* did this? Dragging his victim around Troy's walls in a brash insult to King Priam? I forgot his call sign, but that man is my only fictional corollary: his invincibility, his skill at war, his hubris. But for this fact: *I am lacking a hind foot, or any foot part or body part that is frail, so I am totally without a flaw. No man who is born of woman can vanquish this Author!*

You know which guy I'm talking about! What do you call him? If you draw it out, it's "A chill _'s." And if you sound it out, it's "I kill_'s." I kill *whats?* I kill *blanks?* Oh, this is going to stick in my mind all day, until I think of it. If you can fill in blanks with your crayon (as any child worth his salt can), you'll know who I'm talking about.

Lacking a carcass, I must still plan a burial ritual for him, without a physical body. So I find a good plot (a burial plot, not a story plot, which I am still looking for), not far from a highway, in a sort of ditch. It's a bit swampy, possibly, but that's all I'm willing to pay for (As long as Ovid won't mind sharing a tomb with a poor soul or two). Ovid's tomb sits, waiting for his body to inhabit it.

Body and spirit, two opposing things, without any possibility of unification. An antinomy. "Or is it?" you might say. Am I assuming too much dualism—acting Puritan, as Aaron is? "Why not just say 'It's all natural, it's all good,' and drop this dualism stuff? Physics can find no basis for justifying spirituality."

But in my world, in my book, dualism is not just an assumption; it is a physical fact. By my count, Ovid has run into two ghosts so far—a Ghost of Christmas Past, and a Ghost of Christmas Not-Too-Long-Ago. But what about that futuristic ghost—that ghost who, in *A Christmas Carol*, brings about a catharsis for its wary protagonist? Bah, humbug! Ovid too is a ghost, vanishing from our story. And without Ovid, my story has no conclusion—no "third act" to bring back his past and stir up his dormant passion, and joy of living.

I am giving up on Ovid. I am not looking for him. I am raising a wall against him. I am pushing Ovid out of my story. I forbid him. And just as God bans Satan from his kingdom for daring to claim parity with him, so will I ban Ovid from my story, and Ovid will go out with a bang.

Now a wall surrounds our loyal four: Cain, Paco, Abraham Lincoln, and Anzora. Shut off from Ovid. A physical boundary. To our right, it blocks off anything past Ohio. Going south, it stops in Arkansas and Oklahoma. But going north, it just follows on and on to untold locations: through Canada, and Alaska, across a strait, straight to Russia, Mongolia, and China, joining with a famous wall that you know about from history class, barring off all barbarian nations and unfamiliar notions. Making limitations and inhibitions and isolation.

I will banish Ovid, abandoning him for good. As soon as I am through looking at his journal....

Four months ago, Cain took Ovid's journal and took a flight back to Montana. But Cain, in typically undutiful fashion, did not look at it. Cain was afraid, though I do not know why. Ovid is not scary. But to Cain, Ovid is a phantom, always lurking just out of his sight.

Cain puts Ovid's journal on his nightstand. Cain walks by it on many occasions throughout his day, but without picking it up. Now and again, Cain sits on his quilt, picks up Ovid's journal, and puts it down. It is as though Cain is mocking his Author. Torturing him with his inactivity. Not again! First my protagonist, and now my dramatic foil! How long can this mutiny go on? I will not bow; I will not fail. If I must launch an attack on two fronts, I am willing to do so. I am not afraid! I will kill you all! This Author has no qualms about vanquishing his fictional world's population—man, woman, and animal. (Though, as I said, I will not kill kids, fictional or actual.)

Cain! Do it now! I command you! Do not join Ovid in his vain pursuit of glory, and his illusions of grandiosity! Pick up his book and flip through it. Now! Or I will undo you.

Thankfully, Cain is not as stubborn as Ovid. Cain looks up to God, his Author, finding my words within him, and acting accordingly. Summoning a stalwart spirit, Cain picks up Ovid's journal and cracks its binding. Now, as Cain flips through it, I am looking on....

It has no pagination. No margins. No notations. Just rows and rows of words, from top to bottom, as though Ovid was writing down his thoughts on a papyrus scroll, moving his quill quickly across it, without stopping.

Ovid's journal is chaotic, uncontrollably so. It is full of phantasmagoria—imagistic words and wordy drawings—an audiovisual display of virtuosity, as though wrought by a fit-ful somnambulist, in a flurry of inspiration (or fighting a bout of hypnosis).

For Ovid's journal is not a normal diary, full of gossip and small facts about his daily activity. It is a catalog of books that Ovid was planning on writing, but could not find hours in a day for. A list of thirty-six books, with photographic illustra-tions (four by six, all in full color), fills it.

But, oddly, this compilation of non-books adds up to a book of its own—a quasi-book full of summary and synopsis, half-story, a stop-start narrativity, an almost-plot. It is not just a journal about his book. It is his book.

What is disturbing is that this book of Ovid's is fantastic. It is astonishing. It is a book I would want to Author. It is daunting just to know that Ovid can do this. It boils my blood. Ovid is a fiction! What sad irony this is—that my fictional protagonist could turn out such a work of art whilst I look on, longing for his gifts.

And what is this? This is most unusual. Oddly, Ovid's journal is utilizing an unfamiliar symbol, which looks similar to an "F" laying on top of an "L." His book is full of this symbol, as though it was as common a thing as an "A" or an "I" or an "O."

Oh. Oh....

Now I know! This is how Ovid avoids my Authorial spotlight, though I scan this world with a magnifying glass: through unfamiliar sounds, words, lands, making Ovid privy to all sorts of unknown factors. What did I miss that, having this symbol to draw upon, I might now catch?

I cannot pardon this violation of law. It is a wrongdoing surpassing my capacity for forgiving. Criminal is what it is. You can't just add symbols to a book willy-nilly. It would bring about total anarchy, a dissolution of our linguistic foundations, if anybody who got a notion into his mind could just add symbols and claim that it is only his "grammatical idiosyncrasy." If I allow this, I must allow all individuals within my populous to add symbols at a whim, which I cannot do. Obviously, this is not practical. How would it work? Would a dictionary's author, at that point, just add symbol upon symbol, thus adding word upon word, just to satisfy Ovid's push toward linguistic innovation?

I am at a loss for words. But I can't go losing my words! I am writing a book, and I must finish it! I am God to this world.... I cannot miss a thing. I must consult a dictionary, and put out of mind Ovid's ambition, to look past dictionary-words for unknown words full of unknown symbols. What is a fitting word for Ovid? What kind of diagnosis can I proclaim for him?

Misanthropy: *n.*, A psychological condition in which an individual forms a disliking for all of humanity.

Is Ovid misanthropic? Possibly; but if so, I am misanthropic, too. It isn't such a good diagnosis if it can apply both to you and to your psychologist.

Narcissism: *n.*, A psychological condition for which an individual is fond of nothing but his own individuality.

A-ha! This is it. Ovid is narcissistic. But that is not all. *No, that is not it at all*, Prufrock. Just plain narcissism would not account for Ovid's psychological anomaly. His fatal flaw is not just hubris, but a habit for naval-gazing, a total fixation on his omphalos. What is a word for that?

Solipsism: *n*, A psychological condition in which an individual thinks his own mind is this world's only conscious mind.

All of this, and I still want a word to portray him. That's still not all. Turning back to "Misanthropic," I look down a column or two to its right, and find this word, which fits Ovid to a T:

Moribund: *adj.*, Dying.

Now *that* is a fair portrayal of Ovid. Ovid is dying. For as soon as I can, I will kill Ovid off for good. I'm through toying with him—tossing Ovid around as a cat would a ball of yarn. His doom is an account long outstanding, and it must not go unpaid.

I cannot shut Ovid out now. I must find him, if only to punish him—to bring him pain and discomfort. I am lost in a lack of Ovid, if only as a whipping boy for my story. His truancy is an insult, and I will not shrug it off so lightly.

How can I find Ovid? Put an ad out on a radio station? Ask around at a cocktail party? Pick up hints by word of mouth? Catch him with a booby-trap? Go around sprinkling fairy dust, hoping for a magical solution?

I am looking through Ovid's journal, my fury growing hour by hour, blowing it all out of proportion. How could Ovid think that a fictional man is any match for an Author? How could Ovid turn so quickly into an Author in his own right? And, on top of that, to Author a book surpassing his Author's book? It is a coup, and it calls for military action. But with no combatants to fight against, I am using diplomacy.

Ovid, I am not out to kill you. I am a just and forgiving God. I only want to look upon you again, my child, my only protagonist, "light of my book, product of my brain, my son, my soul—Ovid." How can I stay angry at you? You know I wouldn't hurt you. I was out of control, but I'm OK now. Your running away was hurtful, but you can always turn back to my flock. Ovid! I ask you now: Won't you just turn around, switch back, do a roundabout, and find your way back into our book?

Looking down from my lofty authorial domain, as if on a mountaintop, I watch a man approaching slowly (only a dot from my vista in this cloudy sky). I narrow in upon him. It is Ovid, walking up to our wall with his arms aloft (as though waiting for a hug, or for handcuffs), and standing proud, as though Ovid had anything to act proud about. A portcullis lifts. Crossing a moat, Cain walks out and, taking Ovid in chains, brings Ovid back into our kingdom.

Look at it! It is so faux-mythology, so fantasy-book, so Anglo-Saxon kitsch, it is such a fitting climax for all of our rising action. Visually, it works. But... is that all I had to do? Just ask? Is that all it took? What a disappointing solution, all things told, for Ovid just to walk in by our front door, practically knocking and gaining admission through commanding us to lift our portcullis—making us do his bidding according to his whim. What if I don't want Ovid back in my story? Has Ovid thought of that?

I was starting to think that Ovid would bring about a global manhunt, that Cain would wind up chasing him down a dusty path at a gallop, in hot pursuit of a bad guy in a black hat, as cowboys will do. But now, surprisingly, Cain bumps into Ovid "mano y mano," and brings him in.

Cain looks skyward now, as if to say, "I did it. I brought Ovid to you. Now what, Lord?"

Ovid is back, but not by your doing. Ovid is back of his own autonomous will, which is almost as bad as his going missing to start with. By coming back in his own way, Ovid has won. But Ovid is in my custody now—and is giving up his body and soul for ransom.

Ovid shouts out, "I am not doing it for you! I am against you and your kind— you quasi-playful authors who just want to inflict constant pain on us fictional individuals. Our pain is your joy. Your only motivation is to put it on display."

If you want so badly to follow through in your constant flight from your Author, why go back to him at all, if not for glory—to star in your own book, to stay immortal, if only in a story. Why not just go from point A to point B, using Occam's Razor, to find a straight-most path to walk upon? You talk about wanting to run away from it all, but now you turn back on your word and go back to point A. Why, Ovid?

"I am doing it for Anna, whom you took from this world. Anna was just a walk-on part in your story, a stand-by."

Bystanding is a hazardous activity. You should watch your family, as I watch you, or you risk losing it all.

"But I am not a spy. I will not inflict constant scrutiny on my family," Ovid says, shaking his fist at his Author with a comically dramatic flair.

No. I will do it for you. But no mind, Ovid. Hush, now. This is my only wisdom, my only truth, my motto:

This too shall pass.

Taking Ovid into my fist by his torso, as a child would a doll, I hold him tightly to my bosom. Finally, Ovid is back in my hands! How can I contain him? Ovid must not find his way out again. First, I must knock him unconscious. Thud!

Now, I am moving Ovid—a chit on a Monopoly board—to an "unknown location." To Broadway? To B&O Railroad? To First National Bank? No. To jail!

In jail, Ovid is "losing his turn." And I am "just visiting," biding my days. I want to watch Ovid act out his own doom, in play form. I will hold back my fury for now, sit in a chair and applaud, trying to banish from my mind this thought: that as long as Ovid is still living, Ovid has an opportunity to run away; and I cannot kill Ovid until I am through writing this book.

BOOK FOUR

Ovid's Trial

(A Play in Six Acts)

Dramatis Non Grata (Cast):

Officials:
>A solicitor, Man in a Black Coat
>A plaintiff, Corporal Padlock
>A courtroom typist, Abraham Lincoln
>A bailiff, Man and Woman in Uniform
>An assistant bailiff, Woman Out of Uniform
>Your Honor, also in a black coat

Spiritual advisors:
>A Catholic monk in a cowl
>A Buddhist monk in a gown
>A Rabbi studying his Kabbalah
>An Imam in a burka
>A Taoist monk with his Sutras
>A Sufi mystic

Doctors:
>A psychologist
>A psychiatrist
>An ophthalmologist
>A cardiologist
>Dr. Doc, a urologist
>Dr. Quinoa, an OB/GYN

Court participants:
>Harry Math
>Cain
>Paco
>Librarian, Ghost of Christmas Past

Durand Durand, Ghost of Christmas
Not-Too-Long-Ago
Anna, Ghost of Christmas Tomorrow

Man jurists:
Who
What
I Don't Know
Today
Tomorrow
You

Woman jurists:
Whom
Why
I Know
Not Today
How About Tomorrow
You-Know-Who

First Act

[August 2006: Gitmo prison, in Guantanamo Bay, Cuba, out of U.S. jurisdiction. A big room full of various "combatants"—Iraqis (Sunni Arabs, mostly), Talibani, radical Muslims of all kinds. Through a row of bars, Corporal Padlock, a stoic man of about sixty, stands rigidly against a wall. Ovid is lying in a circular patch of dirt, stirring in a pool of mud.]

Ovid: [upon waking up] What's going on? What is this?

Corporal Padlock: [stoically] Hmmph.

Ovid: Oh no. [looking around him, at his surroundings] I'm not in Wisconsin, am I?

Corporal Padlock: This is Gitmo: a naval station, and war prison, in Guantanamo Bay, Cuba.

Ovid: [looking now at his Arab co-captors] Hmmm... I thought that Cuba was primarily Hispanic. [to Corporal Padlock] If this is a prison of war, I must ask, what is my status?

Corporal Padlock: Combatant.

Ovid: But... that's not right, is it? As I am in a prison of war, I'd call my condition that of a P.O.W. Isn't that only fair?

Corporal Padlock: [stoic] No.

Ovid: Can you say *why* I am a combatant, and in military custody?

Corporal Padlock: It is not in my authority to impart that information.

Ovid: Just so I know, though—is it for my radical political outlook? That I am advocating for Canada to join with our nation and form a hybrid country, which is both socialist and militarily strong? Is this a political prison?

Corporal Padlock: [scoffing] All prison is political. [wanting to stop, but cannot hold back] And Canada isn't a country. It's a bunch of Canucks living in a fantasy world. But it's a post-war world now. It calls for a Winston Churchill, not a Chirac or Sarkozy.

Ovid: [to his co-captors] A Francophobic Army man! How original! [to Corporal Padlock] I am a fan of Winston Churchill. But how can you call our country's dictator a "Winston Churchill" with his cowboys-and-Indians, shoot-from-his-hip way of running things?

Corporal Padlock: [cracking a slight grin] It's not so smart to talk politics in prison.

Ovid: [thinking on this, his hand stroking his stubbly chin-hair] A good point.

Corporal Padlock: [grudgingly] But if you insist, I will say that our "dictator," as you call him, is not autocratic. In fact, his plan to attack both Iraq and Afghanistan had full public support.

Ovid: But... a half a million Iraqis! What human cost is this man willing to pay to satisfy his vanity?

Corporal Padlock: [looking indignant] By disparaging our con-
tributions, you would also talk rot about this Man and Woman
in Uniform. [Corporal Padlock, with much showmanship,
points to a man and woman—in uniform—standing in half-
shadow, up against a blank wall.]

Man and Woman in Uniform: [standing tall, talking in
sync] Sir!

Ovid: Thank God! Our troops! My salvation!

Man and Woman in Uniform: [to Ovid] How do you do, Sir?

Ovid: I'm doing horribly, if you must know. I am in this
prison unjustly.

Man and Woman in Uniform: [to Ovid] Sorry to find you in
such poor conditions.

Ovid: [to Man and Woman in Uniform] If your sympathy is
with my plight, can't you allay it? Try to talk Corporal and his
goons out of torturing this poor soul!

Corporal Padlock: [pointing toward Ovid] This man is a combatant, and thinks that our war coalition is just a big sham.

Man and Woman in Uniform: [talking in unison] *This man is a*
combatant, and thinks that our war coalition is just a big sham.

Ovid: It's not so! Don't you form any opinions of your own?

Man and Woman in Uniform: Not as troops, sir.

Corporal: [butting in] Officially, I talk for this pair. What this
actual man and woman think is unimportant. What I think in

my official capacity as a stand-in for this Man and Woman in Uniform, though, is what counts.

Ovid: But what if I want to talk to this Man and Woman in Uniform? I think that this pair might want to talk, man to Man-and-Woman, without your guardianship.

Corporal Padlock: [turning toward Man and Woman in Uniform, and arching his brow] If you wish.

Man and Woman in Uniform: [looking back and forth from Ovid to Corporal Padlock] No thank you.

Ovid: But… now how can I know what is going on in this war, and in this prison? If all I know about my situation is through buzzwords and military propaganda, I can't fully grasp my situation in all its particulars. I can only brood on what awful things might occur. Shouldn't you inform your public? Shouldn't all civilians, by right, know what our military is doing with its combatants (and P.O.W.s, as I am) in its prisons?

Corporal Padlock: [looking anxiously at Man and Woman in Uniform, and back at Ovid] Hush now, or I'll ship you off to Abu Ghraib.

Ovid: Oh, but I am not a good man for torturing. I would say just about anything for you to stop your assault, and anything I say would only confirm your suspicions, arising as it would out of physical pain.

Arab Combatant: [butting in] You talk as though you could launch Jihad. Why don't you join us in our Holy War?

Ovid: Oh, but I am not a good man for martyrdom. I am a pacifist. I must admit, I can't so much as walk into a *church*

154

comfortably, as a wood crucifix hanging on a wall will bring about thoughts of crucifixion.

Arab Combatant: Truly, Allah only asks his martyrs to go out quickly, and not with long, drawn-out spasms of pain. That is only for Christians.

Ovid: [with sympathy] I'm sorry, but Jihad isn't my thing.

Corporal Padlock: [to Man and Woman in Uniform] Watch how quickly Ovid joins our Arab combatants and starts to talk Jihad.

Man and Woman in Uniform: This is making my stomach turn. I can't watch. Our own compatriot is colluding with an Islamic radical!

Ovid: Wait! OK, I *am* talking with a Jihadist, but it is *you* who brought him into my prison. My only sin is that I will talk to anybody. And I am only talking to this holy warrior in a bid to bring my pacifistic ways to his spiritual philosophy. If I could just impart this bit of wisdom to him—that antagonism is not God's way—it might avoid a military conflict and bring lasting stability to Iraq. It's diplomacy!

Corporal Padlock: Not only is Ovid a coward and a traitor, but Ovid is also as dumb as a stump. Diplomacy? Bringing lasting stability to Iraq? Who said anything about bringing stability to Iraq?

Ovid: But wasn't that our motivation for going into Iraq?

Corporal Padlock: Foolish Ovid. Iraq *had* "stability."

Ovid: What was it all for? Oil? Guns? Land?

Corporal Padlock: Stupid, sad Ovid. Our motivation for going into it was always to show our military might, particularly to that world body that claims authority in what is rightfully our domain: control of world affairs. It has nothing to do with "lasting stability."

Man and Woman in Uniform: So, Corporal, you say that this is actually a war on all nations, to unbind our military from UN intrusion, and has nothing to do with Iraq in particular?

Corporal Padlock: [to Man and Woman in Uniform, uncomfortably] I said nothing of that kind. Ovid is using his voodoo again, and causing you auditory hallucinations. Put him in isolation this instant, so that Ovid cannot harm us with his black magic.

[Man and Woman in Uniform drag Ovid out of his prison and into a small, dark room with no windows or light of any kind.]

Act Two

[A small room with no window or light of any kind. Ovid is shaking, curling up into a ball. It is totally dark now, but to Ovid's dismay, a thin ray of light pours out from his door, which is ajar (paradoxically, both a door *and* a jar). From that doorway, a tall man in a black coat walks into Ovid's tiny prison, bringing in a chair, and sits down, facing Ovid.]

Ovid: [stung by bright lights] Who is it?

Man in Black Coat: I am just a man—a man trying to assist you.

Ovid: A spook?

Man in Black Coat: [laughing] A G-man? Hardly.

Ovid: Not FBI, huh? So... what is it? CIA? NSA? NSC?

Man in Black Coat: Wrong, wrong, and wrong. I'm just a U.S. consul working on your trial.

Ovid: Thank God! I *thought* that, as a civilian, I had a right to a lawy—

Man in Black Coat: [cutting in] — whoa, whoa. I am just a consul. I can act as your law consultant, but I can't go to bat for you in court.

Ovid: OK, OK. That's still good though, right? [Anxiously rubbing his hands] So what's on our to-do list for this trial?

Man in Black Coat: First, pick jurists.

Ovid: All right. So who is first on our list of jurists?

Man in Black Coat: That's right.

Ovid: What? I'm asking you who is on first?

Man in Black Coat: Yup. Who's on first.

Ovid: [talking soft and low] This sounds oddly familiar. [to Man in Black Coat] I don't know who is on first. I'm asking *you*. Who's on first?

Man in Black Coat: Right. Who.

Ovid: I don't know!

Man in Black Coat: No, I Don't Know is on third.

Ovid: What?

Man in Black Coat: What is jurist two.

Ovid: But who is on today?

Man in Black Coat: No. Today is on fourth.

Ovid: So if our fourth jurist is on today, who is on tomorrow?

Man in Black Coat: No. Who is on first, Today is on fourth, and Tomorrow is on fifth.

Ovid: I'd laugh if it wasn't all so absurd. Though I will hang for it. What is wrong with you, anyway?

Man in Black Coat: Nothing is wrong with You. You is our sixth jurist.

Ovid: I'm going crazy with all this jargon!

Man in Black Coat: Don't shout, Ovid. I am trying to assist you. I'm doing this pro bono, you know?

Ovid: Pro Bono? Which Bono? Sonny Bono, or just plain old Bono?

Man in Black Coat: Just pro bono.

Ovid: For Bono! That's good for my situation, isn't it? Isn't Bono a human rights activist? Is Bono putting on a rock show for P.O.W.s unjustly stuck in prison?

Man in Black Coat: [ignoring Ovid] I don't usually do pro bono, but this lawsuit's conclusion, as far as I know, is a fait accompli, so it is my duty, a priori, to go quid pro quo. Got it?

Ovid: ...

Man in Black Coat: This is an ad hoc campaign on my part, and as soon as I am out, I will go incognito, and you will go incognito, too. Got it?

Ovid: I don't know what you say, and I don't know if I can trust you, but I am out of options, so I must go along with it.

Man in Black Coat: As Saint Martin said, "Roma tibi subito motibus ibit amor." *For my labors, you will go to Roma, summit of all your pursuits.*

Ovid: [looking down at his dirt floor] I will act as though you didn't just spout palindromic Latin.

Man in Black Coat: OK, I'll put it this way: A famous man—was it Bob Browning?—said long ago that "No man is an island."

Ovid: It wasn't Browning, I don't think. It was brown-ish, though…. Was it Tan? Auburn? Ah, it was Dun! But Mr. Dun is not as famous for his lyrics as Paul Simon, and Paul Simon said, "I am a rock. I am an island."

Man in Black Coat: Paul Simon is a liar. I wouldn't trust him as far as I could throw him. I wouldn't follow him as far as Scarborough Fair. Just as Garfunk—

Ovid: [cutting in]—Did Corporal Padlock bring you in as a form of psychological manipulation? What do you want?

Man in Black Coat: It's not about what I want. It's what *you* want. I am at your disposal.

Ovid: What am I doing in this prison?!

Man in Black Coat: OuLiPoCorp is charging you with anticipatory plagiarism.

Ovid: Anticipatory plagiarism? My book? But it's all original; it's totally original!

Man in Black Coat: Nothing is totally original. And, by accusing you of "anticipatory plagiarism," OuLiPoCorp is not accusing you of ripping it off from anybody in your past. It says that you took your writings from upcoming books—futuristic books that, now, may not occur at all. And OuLiPoCorp says it's all your doing.

Ovid: My doing? That's ridiculous! It's absurd!

Man in Black Coat: Absurdity is our playground. All of us, living in absurdity. But what is truly absurd is your writing a book with no A, I, O, or U in it. What kind of a man would do such a thing? It only sows confusion.

Ovid: What is going on? Do you actually *buy* all this "anticipatory plagiarism" stuff?

Man in Black Coat: I think your word is truth. But it is my job to think so. My job is also to ask you: Will you proclaim "guilty" or "not guilty"?

Ovid: How can I say if I'm guilty or not guilty to such a ridiculous and unfair law?

Man in Black Coat: It's "guilty" or "not guilty." Not almost-guilty. Not possibly-guilty. Just *guilty* or not *guilty*. Got it?

Ovid: Stop saying "Got it"! I got it!

Man in Black Coat: Talk softly, Ovid, and carry a big stick, and you will go far, as FDR said.

Ovid: It wasn't FDR; it was TR. I should know. I'm an armchair historian, and World War II is my focus of armchair study.

Man in Black Coat: OK, smart guy. Who said, "Ask not what your country can do for you; ask what you can do for your country"?

Ovid: JFK! That wasn't hard at all. But JFK had nothing to do with World War II.

Man in Black Coat: JFK? Is that so? I always thought it was LBJ.

Ovid: No. That SOB was MIA as JFK was giving his SOU. LBJ was taking LOA from CDC whilst his CIC was DOA.

Man in Black Coat: Hmmm... Your acronyms don't scan. I was talking Latin, and all you can do is talk acronyms? It's just so many Alpha-Bits in a bowl of milk.

Ovid: LOL-LMAO-ROFL.

Man in Black Coat: [talking to nobody in particular, as Groucho Marx will occasionally do] Now Ovid is just making stuff up.

Ovid: [translating] "Laughing out loud, laughing my ass off, rolling on floor, laughing."

Man in Black Coat: [with disgust] That's not communication.

Ovid: It's 2006. Don't you IM on AOL? MSN?

Man in Black Coat: A-ha! MSN: That's Microsoft, right?

Ovid: It's as though you sit around in a prison all day, staring at walls.

Man in Black Coat: Not so! I watch Cold War sci-fi films all day long.

Ovid: Cold War sci-fi films? I am a fan, too!

Man in Black Coat: You know Robby Robot? Will Robinson? Gort, Klaatu's robot?

Ovid: Klaatu's robot? Naturally, I do.

Both: [talking in unison] "Klaatu Barada Niktu."

Ovid: [noticing Man in Black's proclivity towards social oblivion, which, though similar to his own, will do nothing to sway his jury, thinks, "Warning, Will Robinson! Warning, Will Robinson!"] Oh, my. I am in for a difficult trial.

Third Act

[A courtroom full of OuLiPo. A military tribunal stands in formation. A group of officials, doctors, spiritual advisors, ghosts, and a jury (consisting of six angry man-jurists and six angry woman-jurists) sit all in a row. A hush falls on this crowd as Ovid walks out into its midst.]

Your Honor: Stand up. [All stand]

Your Honor: Now sit down. [All sit]

Your Honor: Stand up. [All stand]

Your Honor: Now sit down again. [All sit]

Your Honor: Again! Stand. [All stand]

Your Honor: Now sit! [All sit]

Your Honor: This is fun! And good for your body, too! Now, Ovid, I know that you had no room to sit or stand for days, so I thought it would do you good. Do you want to do it again?

Ovid: No, thank you, Your Honor.

Your Honor: Now, I don't know much about what's going on with you and OuLiPoCorp, but I'm not big on "traditions" and "laws" and such. How about you and your antagonist go at it right now, man to man, with your fists?

Ovid: I am a pacifist. I won't fight.

Your Honor: [frowning] I'm sorry it has to go this way. A trial is no fun, but a fight is a joyful thing.... OK, Ovid. Guilty or not guilty?

Ovid: Not guilty, Your Honor.

Your Honor: But I didn't say what criminal acts I am charging you with!

Ovid: I think I know. "Anticipatory plagiarism."

Your Honor: Ah, but that is not all. No, that is not it at all. OuLiPoCorp is now accusing you of killing.

Ovid: Killing *whom?*

Your Honor: Anna Dullann. Do you know Mrs. Dullann?

Ovid: I do. I am *Ovid* Dullann. Anna is my missus.

Your Honor: So you admit to knowing this Mrs. Dullann, whom OuLiPoCorp is accusing you of killing?

Ovid: [nods] But I did not kill Anna. It was my Author!

Your Honor: Your Author is not on trial today, Mr. Dullann. I don't want you making accusations. Just say "guilty" or "not guilty."

Ovid: Not guilty, on both counts.

Your Honor: [looking at his watch, sighing wistfully] I wish you would just say "guilty" right now, so I'm not waiting around all day with you complaining about how unfair it is for a military man to act as OuLiPoCorp's solicitor.

Ovid: Your Honor, who is OuLiPoCorp's councilor?

Your Honor: Corporal Padlock.

Ovid: And who is my councilor? [pointing at Man in Black Coat] Him?

[Man in Black Coat throws back his hood, and to Ovid's alarm, Paco jumps down. Paco was riding piggy-back on Cain all throughout this. "Man in Black Coat" was a spy all along, trying to coax an admission out of Ovid from his first word.]

Your Honor: No. That man is a spy working to undo Castro's dictatorship in Cuba from within. You didn't bring your own proxy?

Ovid: I can't afford a council. Can I do this trial on my own?

Your Honor: [with schoolmarmish disdain] I don't know, Ovid. Can you?

Ovid: *May* I?

Your Honor: OK.

Ovid: Thank you, Your Honor. [soft and low] I must say, though, that having a trial with no councilor isn't so fair.

Your Honor: [aghast] What did I just say to you about complaining?

Ovid: But you said that prior to my actual complaint.

Your Honor: [ignoring Ovid] OK. On to our trial. I now call forward Harry Math, a coordinator for OuLiPoCorp, an instructor at Madison Public High School, and prior to that, a writing-school buddy of Ovid's.

Ovid: I wouldn't call him a "buddy," though.

Your Honor: [with aggravation] Call him what you want. Harry is our first court participant.

Harry: Thank you, Your Honor.

Your Honor: Would you sign a contract saying that what you say today is truth, total truth, and nothing but truth?

Harry: I would.

Your Honor: Good.

Corporal Padlock: [approaching Harry] How long did you go to school with Mr. Dullann?

Harry: Just six months. Fall to spring of sixty-six. Ovid was just a kid, and I was graduating.

Corporal Padlock: During that Fall and Spring, was Ovid writing any books?

Harry: Uh-huh. Ovid would always start books. So Ovid was always writing, without finishing anything.

Corporal Padlock: But Ovid did finish a book, no? *Marginalia*, I think it is?

Harry: Hardly. *Marginalia* is simply a bunch of words filling up a book's margins, but it's all blank!

Corporal Padlock: How about you? Did you finish any books during that six-month span?

Harry: Um... no, I did not.

Corporal Padlock: Would you say that Ovid's habit of starting and not finishing books was contributing to a lack of book-writing on your part?

Harry: I would say so.

Corporal Padlock: How can you justify saying that Ovid's writing was inhibiting your own?

Harry: Ovid's productivity was in proportion to my non-productivity. Prior to Ovid's joining our program, I was a prolific author. During his stay at our school, though, my output was nil.

Corporal Padlock: But why?

Harry: Ovid would start so many books, trying out so many ways of writing a story, that nothing was sacrosanct. His stink was upon all kinds of books. It's as though a child, licking a pizza, lays his claim upon food that is not rightfully his.

Corporal Padlock: OuLiPoCorp has a word for this. Two words, actually. Anticipatory plagiarism! Do you know what a major accusation this is?

Harry: I do. But it is so.

Corporal Padlock: Thank you, Your Honor. I am through with my inquiry.

Your Honor: Ovid, do you want to talk?

Ovid: [looking scornfully at Harry] I do.

Harry: Do your worst.

Ovid: Which school did you and I go to?

Harry: Harvard.

Ovid: OK, now just say that my going to school with you at Harvard was hurting your writing. Couldn't you just up and go to Iowa, or Johns Hopkins, or Brown?

Harry: Brown? [shaking off that insult] That is missing my point. Having known you, I cannot now author books of any kind, as your promiscuous writing pursuits occupy all paths. You put up a roadblock for my writing.

Ovid: If, as you say, I cannot finish books that I start, why not just do it on your own, and in a way that will far surpass my original?

Harry: It's that pizza analogy again.

Ovid: In your pizza analogy, licking a pizza is tantamount to plagiarism?

Harry: Uh-huh.

Ovid: So what, in this analogy, is an act of masticating a pizza, or swallowing a pizza?

Harry: I didn't think it out that far.

Ovid: What if "licking" a pizza is analogous to "just trying a story out," and "masticating" a pizza is an act of "anticipatory plagiarism," and "swallowing" it is actual "plagiarism," In this analogy, am I still practicing "anticipatory plagiarism" as your accusation says I am?

Harry: That's not fair. It's circular logic!

Your Honor: Hold on now, Ovid. I must butt in. It is important, in this court, that you mind this fact: I am a strict constructionist. Do you know what that is?

Ovid: [shrugging] That, in addition to judging in this court, you strictly work in construction?

Your Honor: Hardly.

Ovid: Is it similar to a social constructivist?

Your Honor: Not at all... though possibly so, now that I think about it. It is a judicial philosophy that honors actual words, and not just implications. It is important for you to know that I am using our Constitution as a basis for law, and not "natural law," or what our Constitution's original authors *might want*, if around today. Do you know Antonin Scalia?

Ovid: Oh no. Antonin Scalia! Is Your Honor a Scalian?

Your Honor: Not totally. I am a bit Scaly, but not fully Scalian. Anyway, Scalia is a strict constructionist, as I am.

Ovid: So how is this "anticipatory plagiarism" law put down in books, so I can go about utilizing "actual words" from law, and not just implications?

Your Honor: Ovid, if you wish to act as your own councilor, you must do your work, and not ask this court how a law is put down. It is your job now to find out.

Ovid: But how can I, if I am stuck in a tiny prison with no light, and no room to sit or stand?

Your Honor: That's for you to work out.

Ovid: If that is so, I am without options. I must act upon implications, and not original construction.

Your Honor: I cannot allow it. That is judicial activism!

Ovid: But I am not judging. Your Honor is.

Your Honor: Good. I thought you'd forgot that.

Act Four

[Guantanamo Bay, Cuba: A courtroom at mid-day. It is April First; Ovid's fifty-first birthday. A high window allows a wan ray of light through, if faintly. A jurist up front is nodding off. Four out of six doctors—a psychiatrist, a psychologist, a podiatrist, and a chiropractor—all stand arm to arm in front of Your Honor.]

Corporal Padlock: What do Four Out of Six Doctors say about Ovid's situation.

Four Out of Six Doctors: Four Out of Six Doctors say that Ovid is guilty.

Your Honor: So that's that. Thank you, Doctors.

Ovid: [talking out of turn] But... that's just a group of MDs that OuLiPoCorp found in a psychiatric ward in Bumfuck, Ohio! What about my trial by jury?

Your Honor: Mr. Dullann, what this group of doctors has to say is totally apropos to this court. Authority is our last bastion against anarchy. What is it, Ovid? Don't you *trust* Four Out of Six Doctors?

Ovid: To pick my toothbrush, possibly, but not in moral affairs! Anyway, this group of quacks didn't so much as study my foot.

Corporal Padlock: Should I only bring up doctors who did study your foot?

Ovid: As long as it is a podiatrist who knows my history, and who is from my town and country, at minimum.

Corporal Padlock: OK. I now call forward Dr. Quinoa, an OB/GYN from London, and I call forward Dr. Dock, your urologist.

[Four Out of Six Doctors sit back down, and two out of six doctors—Dr. Dock and Dr. Quinoa—stand up.]

Ovid: [pointing at Dr. Quinoa] That is not my doctor. I don't know that man.

Corporal Padlock: Ah! But that man knows *you*, Ovid. Dr. Quinoa was your OB/GYN. Dr. Quinoa brought you into this world, as an infant, long ago. His touch was your first human touch out of your mama's womb.

Ovid: What could my OB/GYN possibly bring to light about this trial?

Your Honor: Ovid, wait your turn. You must hold your inquiry until Corporal Padlock is through talking with Dr. Quinoa.

Corporal Padlock: Thank you, Your Honor. Dr. Quinoa is a busy man, so I will just ask this: As Ovid's OB/GYN, do you think about Ovid now and again?

Dr. Quinoa: I do.

Corporal Padlock: Hmmm... Now, Dr. Quinoa, can you justify why you—an old OB/GYN who has brought thousands of infants into this world—would find occasion to think now and again about this particular infant from long, long ago?

Dr. Quinoa: As an infant, Ovid was my first no-baby.

Corporal Padlock: I'm sorry... a *no*-baby?

Dr. Quinoa: [nodding] Only a singular baby out of a thousand infants born into our hospital is what I call a no-baby: an intrinsically malicious and naturally bad baby. Ovid was such a baby.

Corporal Padlock: How do you know how to spot such a baby?

Dr. Quinoa: A baby's usual proclivity is to root for its mommy's bosom, suckling at it, cooing happily as it has its first food. But a no-baby looks this way and that, all shifty, not focusing on anything in particular, and is almost plotting his first kill from his crib.

Corporal Padlock: Dr. Quinoa, is such a baby in this courtroom today?

[Dr. Quinoa nods]

Corporal Padlock: Can you point out this baby to us?

Dr. Quinoa: [pointing at Ovid] That's him.

Corporal Padlock: [smiling viciously] Your turn, Ovid.

Ovid: Dr. Quinoa, I am just curious, what is your spiritual background?

Dr. Quinoa: Nothing. I'm from London, so officially I'm Anglican.

Ovid: So, is it a part of your capacity as an OB/GYN to draw conclusions about spiritual affairs?

Dr. Quinoa: No. But I know a bad baby from a good baby.

Ovid: You know this through intuition? Is dividing good and bad infants your official domain of authority?

Dr. Quinoa: No, it is not.

Ovid: [smiling victoriously] I'm through with my inquiry, Your Honor.

Your Honor: All right. I now call forward Dr. Dock.

[Dr. Dock stands up]

Your Honor: Would you sign a contract about truth and so on?

Dr. Dock: I don't know. I'd want to look at this contract first.

Your Honor: Oh, it's not that important. Go on.

Corporal Padlock: Dr. Dock, how do you know Mr. Dullann?

Dr. Dock: I am his urologist at Madison Public Hospital in Madison, Wisconsin.

Corporal Padlock: So you can claim an intimacy with Mr. Dullann that nobody but his missus can, is that right?

Dr. Dock: That's right.

Ovid: [butting in] How so?

Corporal Padlock: [turning to Ovid] In this way: that Dr. Dock has had his hands on your putz.

Ovid: I hardly think that "putz" is using clinical vocabulary. And how is all of this significant to my guilt or lack of guilt in this trial?

Corporal Padlock: I am trying to show your motivation for killing Anna. [turning toward Dr. Dock] During 2002 to 2006, did Mr. And Mrs. Dullann shtup at all?

Dr. Dock: No.

Ovid: That's not so! How would this quack know anything about that? And what's with all this Yiddish? Isn't all this slang unfit for this court?

Your Honor: Ovid is right. But I find it amusing. Carry on.

Corporal Padlock: How do you know that Ovid and Anna didn't, um, "do it"?

Dr. Dock: Ovid's putz didn't work as it should. From 2002 to 2006, Ovid would visit my hospital and ask for Viagra, always upping his quantity from month to month. I would fill out his script, and it still wouldn't do anything for his dysfunction.

Ovid: I can justify that! Long ago I got a spam mail saying, "Buy Viagra," which I thought was a drug for chronic pain, which I had in my groin. This was in 2002, prior to Viagra's surging popularity in spam-mail circuits—

Your Honor:—I don't know if I want to know all about Ovid's marital history—

Ovid: So anyway, I go to my local pharmacy to buy Viagra, and this pharmacist says, "Go ask your doctor for a script." So I go ask my urologist—Dr. Dock—and my urologist says, "So what's wrong with your putz?" So I say, "I'm having groin pain, and I want Viagra." And *voilà*!

Your Honor: Mr. Dullann, why did you maintain your script through 2006, if you got your original script in 2002?

Ovid: I can justify that, too. At first, this Viagra stuff was disappointing. My pain wasn't going away; I was sluggish, and vomiting at night. But I soon found out that, with this drug, I could walk around all day with a hard-on.

Your Honor: Didn't you worry about symptoms such as your hair coming out, or loss of vision, or your digits falling off?

Ovid: All I thought about was my hard-on, Your Honor. If I may ask, Your Honor, how did this court obtain my urologist as a participant in this trial?

Your Honor: It wasn't hard. [Your Honor laughs, and Corporal Padlock joins in]

Ovid: Your Honor is making fun now. I don't think—

Corporal Padlock: [cutting in]—I'm sorry, Your Honor. I was just asking Dr. Dock about his official position on Ovid's condition.

Your Honor: Go on, Corporal.

Corporal Padlock: Dr. Dock, what is your official position on Ovid's ability to maintain a hard-on?

Dr. Dock: My official diagnosis is that Ovid is cripplingly soft and unfit for manhood.

Ovid: What absurdity! Naturally I'm not hard if I'm visiting my doctor. If I had a raging hard-on all day, I would go soft as soon as I'd walk through your hospital door, wouldn't I?

Your Honor: [looking doubtful] But Dr. Dock is a urologist, and an authority on this topic.

Ovid: [standing up and unbuttoning his pants] Look, do you want proof?

Your Honor: No thank you, Ovid. You may sit.

Corporal Padlock: [to Ovid] Go for it. Why not? [to Your Honor] It's not as though this is our first act of public humiliation in Guantanamo prison.

[stopping mid-zip, scanning this courtroom for a lady worthy of a masturbation fantasy, Ovid's sight falls upon a court bailiff, Woman Out of Uniform, with a midriff-baring suit on.]

Ovid: [looking coy] I'm sorry. Could I ask you to assist?

Your Honor: Assistant Bailiff, would you mind singing "Happy Birthday" to our man on trial? It actually is his birthday, and it's probably his last.

[Ovid looks up at Your Honor with horror]

Woman Out of Uniform: OK, I'll play Marilyn. But what is my motivation?

Your Honor: You just had an affair with JFK.

Woman Out of Uniform: Oh, I know JFK. "Ask... not... what your cunt—"

Your Honor:—All right, all right. Just go on with it.

Woman Out of Uniform: [focusing chi inwardly] First, I must inhabit Marilyn's skin.

Corporal Padlock: I think our assistant bailiff is taking this task too importantly.

Your Honor: It's a good show, Corporal. Don't ruin it now.

[stripping down to what you might call a "birthday suit," Woman Out of Uniform starts singing "Happy Birthday" to Ovid]

Woman Out of Uniform: Happy birthday to you. Happy birthday to you. Happy birthday to Ah-vid.
[Ovid stands up and points to his crotch, showing his unit pushing up against his pants.]

Woman Out of Uniform: [stopping mid-song] So it is a happy birthday for you, isn't it?

Ovid: [to Your Honor] Should I do a "full monty," or not?

Jury: [in unison] Not!

Corporal Padlock: Go for it, Ovid! Without proof, I will go on thinking you can't do it. If you stop now, you will only confirm our worst suspicions.

Dr. Dock: [to Your Honor] That's not Ovid's putz. It's an impostor! I saw him stuff a banana down his pants prior to this trial. Go on and show him, Ovid.

Ovid: Why would I stuff a banana down my pants, not knowing that my urologist would start throwing out such accusations?

[sighing, Ovid unzips and is about to pull down his pants, but Your Honor stops him.]

Your Honor: [looking away from Ovid] Stop! A protrusion in your pants is satisfactory proof of your ability to maintain a flag at full mast.

Ovid: Thank you, Your Honor.

Corporal Padlock: [with a sigh] I don't know what to say. I'm through with my inquiry.

Ovid: [sitting down] I, too, do not know what to say. Not to Dr. Dock and not to Corporal Padlock. His inaccuracy in making accusations about my putz could aptly stand for OuLiPoCorp's inaccuracy in making accusations about my killing Anna. [to Corporal Padlock] What can you do now, for proof of my guilt? You know, and I know, that killing Anna was my Author's work. And this "anticipatory plagiarism" stuff is just your poor way of trying to commit my words to dust. Bring in a thousand doctors if you want. I am not guilty, and I am not afraid. What can you do? What can you do now?

Fifth Act

[Your Honor, Corporal Padlock, and Ovid stand in a triangular formation around Durand Durand's ghost, which is floating up high, forming a triangular prism (or—if you count Woman Out of Uniform, standing slightly away—a pyramid), which sight, until Durand lands in his chair, cannot avoid having a Masonic flair. Six spiritual advisors sit by idly: a Catholic monk in a cowl, a Buddhist monk in a gown, a Rabbi studying his Kabbalah, an Imam with his Quran, a Taoist monk with his Sutras, and a Sufi mystic in a turban.]

Your Honor: Would you sign a contract—

Durand Durand:—I am a ghost. You'd think I could avoid contracts now that I am an amorphous soul with no physical body.

Your Honor: OK, but will you talk truthfully?

Durand Durand: Truthfully, I will talk.

[Your Honor shrugs]

Corporal Padlock: You saw Mr. Dullann prior to your dying on a skydiving trip last May, is that right?

Durand Durand: That's right.

Corporal Padlock: Did Ovid try to stop you in your suicidal jump?

Durand Durand: No.

Corporal Padlock: Ah. So Ovid did not try to stop you from jumping?

Durand Durand: I just told you. No.

Corporal Padlock: OK. So... you saw Ovid again, just six months ago, in your ghost form; is that right?

Durand Durand: That's also right.

Corporal Padlock: And what did Ovid say?

Durand Durand: Ovid said that his mission was to fashion a lipogrammatic book, honoring my own.

Corporal Padlock: Did Ovid author such a book?

Durand Durand: No. First, Ovid was writing about a magician, Dirty Dick, who did sick things to kids, such as cutting his assistant in half. And in Louisiana, Ovid was writing a Civil War story about a woman in a man's body, who turns into a sort of Joan of Arc. Ovid would soon abandon both lipograms, in disgust at his own filthy mind.

Corporal Padlock: What about Ovid's journal; is *that* a lipogram?

Durand Durand: Not by my standards. A lipogram would omit symbols or words, limiting linguistic capability by shutting down our automatic word-manufacturing mind, thus loosing our unconscious. But by adding symbols, Ovid is writing an anti-lipogram, showing a total lack of constraint. It is a crass ploy, a tricky tool, show-offy stuff.

Corporal Padlock: So, in opposition to his vow, Ovid took up a book which was, in your opinion, suspiciously familiar?

Durand Durand: Ovid said outright that it was his plan to author a sinful book, full of moral ambiguity and compromising situations. What I didn't know was that Ovid would author a book that was not only morally but syntactically sinful.

Corporal Padlock: I don't want to stray too far off task. Would you say that Ovid's book is a form of plagiarism?

Durand Durand: I would.

Corporal Padlock: How so?

Durand Durand: Copying words is a form of plagiarism, and so is making up words. Making up words is just a form of copying Our Author, who, through us, is making up our words.

Corporal Padlock: If "copying" words, or "making up," words isn't a hallmark of original writing, what is?

Durand Durand: *Avoiding* words is our only way of writing with any originality. It is in what you or I or Ovid, as authors of our own books, don't (or won't) say that distinguish us from this crowd of card-carrying wordsmiths.

Corporal Padlock: [smugly] Thank you, Durand. I am through.

Your Honor: Ovid?

Ovid: First, Your Honor, may I ask why all this godly authority amongst us? [points to a crowd of monks and rabbis and imams, and so on]

Your Honor: It is armor to ward off ghosts.

Ovid: [quizzically] But isn't Durand Durand a ghost? And isn't Durand Durand a participant in this court?

Your Honor: It will guard us against *bad* ghosts.

Ovid: How many ghosts do you think will show up today?

Your Honor: Only two.

[Shaking off this shadowy thought, Ovid walks up to Durand Durand's ghost, pausing]

Ovid: Did I fail you, Durand?

Durand Durand: I am in limbo now, waiting for you to fulfill your mission.

Ovid: Is that good or bad?

Durand Durand: Limbo is just... nothing.

Ovid: So, it's boring?

Durand Durand: [nods] As boring as an old-folk's club in a run-down community building gymnasium. Nothing to do all day but play ping-pong, tango- or salsa-dancing, and naturally, lots of limbo.

Ovid: Do you think that part of your motivation for standing at this trial is to avoid not words, but doldrums? I know that living (or not living) in limbo is a humdrum thing (or no-thing), but must you cross a physical-spiritual boundary just for a bit of stimulation?

Durand Durand: Accusations? An accusation from you is practically an admission of guilt. If that is all you know how to do, Ovid, I don't know how you think you will avoid prison.

Ovid: Avoid! Avoid! Why is it always "avoid" with you? What is it that you want to avoid?

Durand Durand: I want what you want: to avoid my Author. All of us do. I don't want an Author watching all my actions and guiding my will. A lipogram is a trap door on our world's platform—our only way of taking flight without wings—and without this hatch, all you can do is copy and mimic what your Author wants.

Ovid: But isn't it a kind of lipogram to omit A, I, O, and U from my book's vocabulary, as I did?

Durand Durand: Substituting a funny symbol for A, I, O, and U is not a way of uprooting minds, or taking flight; it is simply a way of codifying your corruption. A word is just a blot of ink on a book, or a sound from out of a baboon's mouth. A non-word—talking around a word and thus nullifying its capacity for signification—is a psychotic act; a call to arms from an anarchic subconscious.

Ovid: If you put it that way, I must admit that my book was not a call to arms from an anarchic subconscious. But... "anticipatory plagiarism"?

Durand Durand: I am not saying that I am going along with OuLiPoCorp. I'm just saying that you did not fulfill your vow, and for that, I am languishing in limbo.

Ovid: [pausing] Thank you, Durand. [to Your Honor] I'm through with this ghost.

Your Honor: I now call forward Anna Dullann.
[Anna's ghost surrounds this courtroom, instilling it with calm, for an instant, as Ovid looks in thrall at this phantom moving across to a chair to Your Honor's right. Anna's ghost has a flowing gown that looks just as Anna's nightgown did, and Anna's ghost has a pallor that is similar to Anna's pallor in living form.]

Anna's Ghost: [waving a ghost hand] Don't ask if I will sign a contract. Don't worry. I will only say that which conforms to truth.

Your Honor: OK. [to Corporal Padlock] Go on.

Corporal Padlock: Mrs. Dullann. Did you and your husband "do it" at all from 2002 to 2006?

Anna's Ghost: I want to talk to Ovid.

Corporal Padlock: But—

Anna's Ghost:—I want to talk to my husband! [a ghost's vocal chords must grow in pitch during immortality, for Anna's roar falls upon this court as a lightning-bolt upon a mountain-top]

Corporal Padlock: I'm through, Your Honor.

Your Honor: [smirking] You can say that again. Ovid, your turn.

Ovid: [falling into a bowing position] Anna!

Anna's Ghost: How could you do it, Ovid?

Act Six

[Ovid walks up to Your Honor and sits in a chair abutting Your Honor's chair. Corporal Padlock stands by, hungrily awaiting his opportunity to grill Ovid, as a suburban dad at a local BBQ might hungrily await an opportunity to grill a pork chop.]

Corporal Padlock: [to Ovid] Writing is cannibalistic, a swallowing of your own kin. How can you do it?

Ovid: If writing is a sin, I am guilty.

Corporal Padlock: So you admit your guilt!

Ovid: No, I said *if* writing is a sin, I am guilty.... It is a conditional admission.

Your Honor: *Is* writing a sin, Corporal?

Corporal Padlock: Hmmm... I don't know. I'm not a Biblical scholar.

Your Honor: But you did go to Sunday school.

Corporal Padlock: [looking to a monk and a rabbi for approval] OK.... Thou shalt not worship idols... thou shalt not kill... [counting on his digits] thou shalt honor thy Lord's Sabbath day... thou shalt honor thy mom and dad... thou shalt not want what thou hast not got....

Ovid: Psst! You forgot "Thou shalt pay an annual tax to thy local church."

Corporal Padlock: Did I? Oh, Ovid is making stuff up again! [to Your Honor] So writing is probably not a cardinal sin, but it *is* an ungodly act. Writing fiction—making up a world and populating it with conflict and immorality—is a symptom of a sick, ungodly mind.

Ovid: But making up a world and populating it with conflict and immorality *is* godly! Didn't God, our Author, do just that? How is God's naming of Adam so distinct from my naming of my own protagonist? Or how is God banishing Adam from his kingdom so distinct from my banishing God?

Corporal Padlock: It is distinct from your story in that *God's* story is truth! Truth as shown through holy books and rituals and traditions, lasting from Anno Domini to today. [finding an opportunity to look good in front of this jury] Or... don't you think that Christ's word is truth?

Ovid: [waffling] It's not *un*truth. I just don't think it has any final claim to truth. Look, an anthropologist, coming upon this "Christian" faith, would think it was curious and quaint, but not a dogma to follow. I would just as soon worship Apollo, or Thor, or Buddha, or Allah.

Corporal Padlock: I want this jury to mark that Ovid would just as soon bow down to Allah as to a Christian God.

Ovid: Which is to say, I would not bow down to any God. In my fictional world, I am king. My dominion is without a doubt. If I could, I would stay within my domain.

Corporal Padlock: But your domain is about as grand as a

child's with his toys, playing on imaginary playgrounds, playing at imaginary war, working towards imaginary goals.

Ovid: But *our* world is imaginary. What if our Author is just a pitiful old man sitting in his tiny living room typing out our trials and tribulations in a fit of whimsy? What if God is laughing at us?

Your Honor: [cutting in] I don't know what good it is to throw out such imaginary conditions.

Corporal Padlock: But wait. I want to stick with "what if's" for now. *What if* Ovid is guilty of anticipatory plagiarism? *What if* Ovid is guilty of killing Anna Dullann? Wouldn't you admit that this pomp and bombast of his is simply a distraction from this trial? Is Ovid so partial to avoid prison that Ovid is willing to ruin our faith in God?

Ovid: It's not my fault that your faith in God is so quick to ruin.

Corporal Padlock: [scornfully] What fatuous opinions you must hold in that corrupt brain of yours.

Ovid: And what vacuous a mind that would call human curiosity a form of corruption.

Corporal Padlock: Such fatuity!

Ovid: Such vacuity!

Corporal Padlock: Fatuous!

Ovid: Vacuous!

Your Honor: [pounding] Stop this childish stuff! Both of you! I wish that you two had just fought it out, man to man, to start with, and not wrought all this hostility and rancor. Can I now adjourn this court?

[Corporal Padlock nods]

Your Honor: OK, that's all. Ovid is our last court participant. So, I will now ask both Ovid and Corporal Padlock for last words. It is up to this jury now to say if Ovid is guilty or not guilty.

Ovid: That's it? That was my trial? Two ghosts, six doctors, and an old school chum? This is our basis for killing or sparing a man? This is his basis for living or dying? What about my right to a fair trial? I had no warning that it would all unfold this way.

Your Honor: This isn't a trial court, Ovid. It is a military tribunal. I thought you'd known all along.

Ovid: Not at all. But now that you say so, how obvious! Our good Corporal is not a plaintiff at all. It's his job to "pacify combatants," and this "trial" is an inquisition. But if our good Corporal can corporally punish a civilian on rumor and insinuation, this is not truly a trial or a tribunal; it is a dark spot on our civilization.

Corporal Padlock: Ovid, you say that your right to "a fair trial" was trod upon. That you had no warning. I find that a bit hard to swallow.

Ovid: And I find aspirin hard to swallow. But aspirin is still a fact.

Corporal Padlock: I hold no accountability for your not knowing what this court was about.

Ovid: This is our first point on which I am in accord with you: That you hold no accountability.

Your Honor: I'm sorry if you didn't know what was going on, Ovid. [laying his chin on his fist, looking wistful] Isn't that always how it is, though? Who knows what is going on in this world? [to Corporal Padlock] Now, Corporal, how about your last words?

Corporal Padlock: [standing up high and proud] I proclaim that Ovid is guilty; guilty, as his old writing school buddy Harry Math told us; guilty, as Four Out of Six Doctors told us; guilty, as his own urologist told us; guilty, as Anna's Ghost told us. Guilty of what? Of many things. Guilty of anticipatory plagiarism—taking words out of our mouths (all of our mouths) and gorging on our words in his own book. Guilty of coming up with a symbol that flouts all our grammatical laws—that in fact flouts all of OuLiPoCorp's laws and customs.

Ovid is guilty, too, of killing Anna Dullann's soul. I know this, for I saw Anna's own ghost say so. I know this, for I saw Ovid drown in guilt and bow down in front of Anna's ghost. I know this, for—what gall!—Ovid said that his faith in a Christian God is in doubt, and that his inclination is to worship Allah! What proof of guilt could you ask for but that Ovid is faithful to Muhammad?

But, as you think on Ovid's guilt, I don't want you to think about Ovid and his criminal acts. I want you to think about his victims. Anna, to whom Ovid had a holy obligation, and did not only fail to fulfill it, but sought to kill Anna simply to nullify that bond. Durand Durand, whom Ovid did not stop from jumping to his doom, and who is still waiting in limbo for Ovid to fulfill his vow. God, whom Ovid insults with his doubt, and whom Ovid disdains by claiming parity with him, as Satan did. And You, whom Ovid shuns by focusing so singularly on *his* world and *his* writing, totally ignoring his public.

Anybody who has thought about working on a book, but is holding off for a rainy day, should scorn Ovid for plagiarizing his words, for not giving us an opportunity to author books of our own. Ovid is taking your thoughts straight out of your brains, and using your thoughts to run his writing factory; in turn, Ovid controls your thoughts by convincing you that your mind is not your own. Sounds conspiratorial? Naturally, for Ovid's *is* a conspiratorial mind. Your only way of stopping him is to find him guilty, right now, in this court. If you don't, Ovid will roam this world poaching thoughts, writing sinful books, and killing, killing, killing anybody in his path. Your duty is obvious, and I call upon you to fulfill your duty, as Ovid could not fulfill his.

Your Honor: Thank you, Corporal. And Ovid? Any last words?

Ovid: [tugging at his collar, looking anxious] Last words? Why call it "last words"? It sounds so morbid. Why not "final summary," or "closing thoughts"?

Your Honor: OK, Ovid. "Closing thoughts." Got any?

Ovid: I'm not guilty. But I'm also not *not* guilty. Do you know what I'm saying? [cutting in on his own thought] No, wait, that's awful; it sounds as though I'm dodging facts with ambiguity. OK, I will say this: It's not as bad as it looks. [cutting in again] No, that's not good. It sounds as though I am caught having an affair. How about this? All of my guilty acts consist of things that you would do, too, if it was you who was doing it. [cutting in] No, no, no. It sounds as though I'm trying to color my guilt with black irony.

Your Honor: Would you hurry it up, Ovid?

Ovid: Sorry, Your Honor. I think I got it… Is this anticipatory plagiarism? "It was a dark and gloomy night…"?

In my opinion it is not. "It was a dark and gloomy night" is such a familiar and awful saying, that I hardly think it worth calling it an "original" work, such that a man can "copy" it. Similarly, my own writing is so awful, it is not worth charging it with plagiarism.

An act of copying only attains plagiarism status if it is also an act of vanity. I don't think that I truly was copying an unknown futuristic book, or copying my own Author (in fact, I was out of my Author's span of vision as I commit my book to writing), but if I was, it is still an act of humility, for my book is humiliating. As I was writing it, my only anticipation was of dishonor and opprobrium, such as it has wrought, and of which this court is proof.

Your Honor: That's it?

Ovid: That's it, Your Honor.

Your Honor: OK. Now our jury can go into a room and concur on your guilt.

[This court's jury walks out through its back door and packs into a small room. A six-man group sits across from a six-woman group, facing off, as though in a showdown. Who, What, I Don't Know, and Today all carry looks of obstinacy. Tomorrow, though, has a dubious look that is, to Ovid, auspicious. You, too, has a look of doubt writ upon it. Doors shut.]

[Six hours pass, and finally, this group of jurists pours out of that room, and hand a slip to Your Honor.]

Your Honor: This jury has not cast its final ballot.

Ovid: Hooray! It's a hung jury!

Jury: Don't try ingratiation with us.

Your Honor: It's not a hung jury, but it hasn't laid down a conclusion to this trial. This jury hasn't found Ovid guilty or not guilty so far.

Corporal Padlock: How is that so? What is not to know?

Your Honor: What knows that Ovid is guilty—or *thinks* Ovid is guilty, I should say. (I almost forgot my impartiality.) But not You.

Corporal Padlock: I know that Ovid is guilty. Who thinks Ovid is not guilty?

Your Honor: No. Who thinks that Ovid is guilty, too. It's You who is not so firm on Ovid's guilt.

Corporal Padlock: I don't know about that.

Your Honor: I Don't Know is with Who and What on this. Ovid is guilty.

Ovid: [to Jury] This again! I think that this plagiarism stuff is our Author's doing—always "quoting" famous sayings, and "paraphrasing" important books. Fiction-writing is all lying and gossip. So what do you say, Author? Stop lurking in shadows, in marginalia, in discursions, and in our subconscious minds! I know it is your hand guiding all of this—Anna, Durand Durand, this court, my psychosis, your absurd and unfair world—so show us a physical incarnation. Stop hiding from us. Talk to us! Author!

FIFTH BOOK

First Part

I am standing in Your jury box. I am lurking in Your vicinity, trying to sway this jury's conclusion by courting Your illustrious opinion. ("I always thought so highly of You. Did You know that? Can I bring you a Fanta? Isn't Ovid guilty?") But jury-rigging is hard to do. Any ruling must by law show total unanimity on all counts. On what topic can *any* random group of six guys and six gals all concur unanimously?

Pacing back and forth, as though I am an official part of Ovid's Trial, I put this inquiry to You and Your co-jurists (talking through Abraham Lincoln, my pawn in this trial): "A show of hands: Who thinks Ovid is guilty?"

"Goddamn right, I do," says Who right away. Who, Whom, What, Why, I-Know, Today, and Not-Today all lift right hands in unison. I-Don't-Know, How-About-Tomorrow, and You-Know-Who shortly follow suit.

Our only holdouts: Tomorrow, our fifth jurist, and You, our

sixth. "C'mon, guys," says I-Know, rocking back on his chair and looking smug.

"Ovid is obviously guilty. Padlock caught him with his pants down, and now Ovid is trying to put on a dog-and-pony show to fool anybody that Ovid can. But I'm not buying it."

Today and Tomorrow start arguing about minor facts from Ovid's trial, quoting from his court transcript. Today is particularly stuck on that instant in which Ovid said, "If writing is a sin, I am guilty."

During a lull, Not-Today adds, "So, Tomorrow. Why don't you join up with us? It's *your* stuff that Ovid is plagiarizing, right? Books of Tomorrow?"

"That's ridiculous," says Tomorrow. "I'm not writing any books. I am an accountant, as Ovid is."

"Tomorrow is an accountant?" How-About-Tomorrow says. "What do you count?"

"What do you think?" says Tomorrow. "I count hours. And I count all man's works and days."

From that point on, it all starts to fall apart, with Today talking on top of Not-Today, and I-Know trying to shout down Why.

Soon, What is smoking a cigar as though nobody told him that you can't light up in a jury room; You-Know-Who wants to stop for lunch; and Whom insists on finding fault with all of Who's grammatical constructions.

I-Don't-Know says, apropos of nothing, "What I want to know is, why isn't this a 'grand' jury? Why am I not a 'grand jurist'?"

Upon absorbing this tidbit of random dialog, Abraham Lincoln walks away from this chaotic situation, throwing his hands up.

Sigh.

As Author, must I always lasso my fictional incarnations, corralling You into my grand plan, as I would a stray foal on a ranch?

Taking You and Tomorrow into a back room, I work my voodoo upon Your pliant minds.

As Mom would say, "If at first you fail, try, try again!" This is my pitch:

If you still think of Ovid as a "good guy," as a "chip off an old block," just look at his son Aaron. What good has Ovid brought *him*? Aaron is only half a man now, with Alyssa torn away from him—his symbiotic twin. His mom cannot comfort him, cannot hold him with two loving arms, cannot sing to him, or tuck him in and fluff his pillow. Anna is rotting away in a coffin. And Ovid is ignoring Aaron, in pursuit of his own ambitions, in flight from his Author, spiraling down into his own paranoia.

Still not of a mind with your co-jurists?

What is wrong with You? Why won't You proclaim Ovid guilty?

You can do it! Clap Your hands if Ovid is guilty! Clap Your hands!

Oh, I know this fairy stuff won't work on *You*. You wouldn't fall for that— anybody who would pick up a big grownup book such as this is too smart for such a childish trick!

But I must warn You. If You think You can avoid this obligation, I'm sorry to say that it is not so. Your duty is unambiguous. This book is not a two-way road. If You start walking on a path towards Ovid's doom, You cannot turn back. You can only put it off for Tomorrow (who is also putting it off for You).

I want to clarify this point, so that no doubt can last in your mind: Your participation was implicit all along. It was You who took on that task: to watch Ovid. It was You who sat idly by, watching Durand Durand fall to his doom, watching Anna succumb to alcoholism and turn victim to Anzora's homicidal ways, watching Ovid run amok, killing his family by cutting it in half! By taking Alyssa away, and abandoning Aaron to Harry Math and his militant Puritanism.

Watching is tantamount to doing. By watching Anna's assassination, and doing nothing to stop it, it is as though You took Konstantinos' gun and shot Anna with Your own hand.

But now I want to thank you: Your habit of watching without infringing upon our story is what finally brings about a ruling of "guilty" for Ovid. By not saying anything, You automatically join with us in proclaiming Ovid's guilt. For You stood by, doing nothing, as so many participants in Ovid's trial said, again and again and again, "Ovid is guilty"!

You, my co-conspirator! You, my complicit spy and collaborator! You, O my soul, my own alibi, and Ovid's downfall and ruination!

Part Two

Now that You know what Your main function is in this story, I will lay it out for you as though from an instruction manual:

You will act as Ovid's jury. You will sway Tomorrow's opinion and stamp out any naysaying as to his guilt. If any doubt should crop up, You will banish it handily by pointing out that Ovid is a known liar and sociopath who can charm anybody with half a mind to follow him. Ovid must not stand trial again. Ovid must vanish, by God's will: by My will, and by Yours.

Naturally, you want my instructions on how to bring about Ovid's final ruin.

Not to worry: I am always full of notions about what kind of harm to inflict upon Ovid. It is critical that Ovid not simply "pass away," but that You sap him of his will to carry on. Ovid cannot just hang; Ovid's agony must prolong so much that Ovid *wants* to hang.

But I must warn You again, it is not simply a natural byproduct of his story, or a curious plot twist on my part. It is a scrupulous act, a plan to trump all plans, a calculation of a highly wrought and painstaking fashion ....

Killing Ovid is an art.

First, Go to Your room—living room, or study; any room will do—pick up a writing tool (or a quill and an inkpot, if you want to do it old school), and sign a sworn affidavit that says, "Ovid is guilty. I saw Ovid kill Anna, and Durand Durand, and Konstantinos. Ovid is an anticipatory plagiarist, and a liar. You cannot trust a word that Ovid says."

Put this affidavit in Tomorrow's hands, and pass it around to all Your co-jurists. Shout it out, if You want: "Ovid is guilty!"

That is all that Tomorrow is waiting for—to go along with You! To follow *Your* path.

Simon says: "Ovid is guilty!"

Now Ovid's jury is unanimous! Congratulations! His ruling is guilty on all counts!

Two: Walk straight into his prison and look right into Ovid's dark, vacant pupils. Ovid is about to go on his last walk, and Ovid knows it. Ovid will, pitifully, hold up a sign that says, "Fictional rights for fictional individuals!" But, though Ovid may start to gain Your sympathy, You must not admit his humanity. Laugh at him. Think of him as a lab assistant would think of a lab rat. Ask, with a patronizing air, "What about fictional rights for non-fictional individuals? Don't non-fictional individuals want fictional rights, too?" This will throw Ovid into a bout of confusion lasting for days. Using this opportunity, go on to our third instruction:

Third, draw Ovid into your flock. At this point, You know that Ovid is full of fantasy and illusion, and You can dismiss his claims out of hand. Maintain Your cool—it is good that Ovid thinks of You as his ally, though Your loyalty is in fact with His Author. For as long as Ovid thinks that it is just You and Him, Him and You: a fictional individual and his non-fictional public, up against a tyrannical Author with an unusually brutal disposition, Ovid will bring You into his trust, and You can draw him in, until Ovid is fully caught within Our trap.

Four: Vilify Ovid in print. Don't worry about portraying "truth," which is such a poor abstraction anyway; just say that Ovid is guilty and say it again, and again, so that it starts to *sound* factual, out of plain familiarity. Bring Your words to Our fictional population. Cry it out

amidst a busy urban crowd. Start a blog. Post to random digital discussions. Mail out a round of spam. Shout it from a rooftop: "Ovid is guilty!"

Fifth, turn Ovid's own ghosts against him. I did it, during his trial, and it was my crowning glory. Did you watch Ovid as Anna took a stand at his trial? His pallor! His bowing and kowtowing—all for that non-living woman, who was fictional to start with! You would think that Ovid saw a ghost, and You would think right (Good job, You!).

As soon as You turn Ovid's ghosts against him, Ovid will finally succumb, caving in to his spiritual wounds. Ovid is compliant, now, with his own doom.

Six (and last): Sit back and savor Ovid's long, torturous road to his own undoing. Don't worry about Ovid's kids—Aaron or Alyssa—and don't wait around for Your humanity to kick in with all of its accompanying pangs of guilt. Just shrug it off and switch it back to Your original programming: "Your Show," starring Ovid Dullann, a clown good only for an occasional laugh. And all of Ovid's props and sight gags won't stop his balloon-string from drifting up, up, and away.

That is My formula for undoing Ovid. Follow it as faithfully as You would follow a cookbook by Julia Child. Do as Romans

do. As I always say: "If you join up with a clan of cannibals,
You ought to act a glutton."

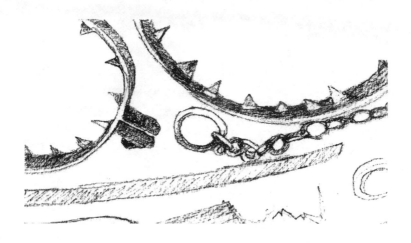

Third Part

Our courtship was a whirlwind affair, wasn't it? Stars in our vision. Visions of sugarplums dancing in our minds. Fluff at first sight. But now all of that is in our past. You and I know what it is to look back on a long cohabitation and think of what a joyous span it was!

For now, I just want to look at our past, and fondly think of *us*:

How about that Ovid? Didn't you just savor his discomfort during his trial, watching him squirm around in his chair as a worm would on a hook?

What, don't you want to talk about Ovid? What's that you say? All I do is talk about Ovid? Ovid-Ovid-Ovid!

Possibly you don't know how an Author could glory in his protagonist's final annihilation. But You will. Oh, I *know* that You will. You know that book you can't stop thinking about? You know! That book that You plan to commit to words as soon as You can go on a long vacation from Your lousy job (I'm assuming Your job is lousy, but what job isn't)? Just wait.

That book, too, is full of anguish, and not just that of Your protagonist.

Anguish is our only topic. I study Anguish. I got my Doctor of Philosophy in Anguish. I call my foot Anguish. My mouth is Anguish. I am sick with it. My Anguish is foot-in-mouth. My Anguish is mad cow. My anguish is -bola and -coli and small pox and all-pox. My hobby: Anguish. My addiction: Anguish. My patron saint: St. Anguish.

"I'm sorry to say that your job application is not up to our standards of quality." Anguish!

"I am writing to inform you that our bank is finalizing your bankruptcy." Anguish!

"I don't know if this is working out. You and I ... it's just not right." Anguish!

"How can I put this? Your diagnosis isn't promising." Anguish!

But all is not lost! You can occupy Anguish as You would a building. You can don a coat of Anguish as a silk gown. If You didn't want Anguish, why did You pick up this book or succumb to this Author? Anguish is all that I supply.

Wait! Don't go! I'm sorry, I will "work on" my Anguish habit. I can act happy, or I can do a passing imitation of happy—look!

You and I should start this up again. You and I should try dating first, and slowly build up to matrimony. Or, hold on; don't think of nuptials just now—think of us as two ships passing at night (or as two cars colliding on a highway). Act as though You don't know who I am, and I too will act as though I don't know You.

I will put out an ad on Craigslist:

You: A young (or old) woman (or man), who will soon finish (or not) this book and who is looking for an Author with irrational moods and abnormal fixations. Must know how to sustain long discussions on fictional topics. Good with imaginary animals. Not too suspicious, or prying, or curious.

How about a walk in a park, and dining out at a local Italian bistro? Or staying in, and watching a romantic film? I can't go *with* you, but you just carry on, and I'll sit around in my study all day, manufacturing fictional individuals in fictional towns with fictional situations. Sound good?

Hmmm … that's too many words. It will cost too much. How is this: "Minor Author looking for book-loving public. Must know how to withstand a constant assault of words, and must want to constantly think about things that just ain't so"?

I know, I am glossing an important part of our courtship: first contact. Arranging a location (not too fancy, not too shabby). Picking You up at Your door, bringing a gift (nothing too rich, nor too shabby), and kissing You awkwardly on Your hand, as I would royalty. Trading coy looks across a lazy Susan, or a bowl of popcorn, or a barstool.

Can't You and I skip all that stuff? Isn't it all just a big mating ritual anyway? Why would a man and woman go out and doll up and act stupid, if not to hook up? It's all a fanciful drama pointing to our animal inclination toward wanton copulation, which is just our roundabout way of bringing about a slight uptick in our population statistics.

You can hold onto Your hoity-toity Puritan notions if You wish. I wouldn't go to any fancy-schmancy dancing hall, or artsy-fartsy gala party. I am a practical man. I go straight for hanky-panky. And I will put on a condom (contrary to my biological motivator, I do not want to add to our human population), and I will do my thing until it falls off. Man or woman. Human or animal. Living or not.

"If it has a slit, I'll stick my prick in it." That's my motto.

(I am sorry if I am "blowing my load" without finishing You off first. An organism's orgasm is its own account, I say. And I'm not fond of cuddling.)

I avoid crowds. I shun hip to-dos and social affairs. I spurn mass actions, flash mobs. So how can I avoid this dating ritual that You insist on taking part in?

I know what I'll do. I will brush You off! I find it most gratifying associating with fictional incarnations anyhow. So, I will put You out of mind for now, and turn back to Ovid:

How should Ovid go out? With a bang? Shall I bring in a firing squad, to shoot him, filling his body with plugs of hot iron, puncturing his skin and organs? Should I bring in an assassin to cut along his jugular, stopping all blood-flow to his brain? Should I kill Ovid as Parisian crowds did with King Louis long ago, guillotining him in a public display of common man's triumph (again, divorcing Ovid's body from his brain)? For it is Ovid's brain, at bottom, which is most at fault. That odious brain, which has brought about such chaos and calamity in our world.

What about an old-fashion gallows? I was always fond of gallows, so what do You think of this particular way of disuniting Ovid from his malignant mind? Gallows humor always draws a laugh! Ovid standing on a scaffold with a hangman is funny. A trapdoor sprung, and Ovid hanging from a gallows until this strangulation kills him—this too is funny! Think of it: Ovid, hung from a gallows until his body grows black and bloats out and starts to stink, and You, hacking away at his hanging body as a child at a birthday party would with a piñata. For sport. For laughs. For a half-hour's worth of distraction.

No. It is only fitting that Ovid is hung from a crucifix. My book is lacking a Christ-symbol, and Ovid will do, with his facial hair from all his months in captivity.

☾

Ovid is sitting in prison, anxiously anticipating his crucifixion. A cross awaits him. Two nails, two planks of wood, and a crown of thorns. Oh, I know that Ovid is "a sitting duck." I know that killing Ovid is "taking candy from a baby." I know that a fictional man is no match for an Author. Still, I long to watch.

What do You think? Will it kill Ovid instantly, through loss of blood? Or will Ovid flail around and spasm, dying gradually by thirst or starvation? Inquiring minds want to know! This waiting stuff is too much. Kill Ovid now!

Do it, You!

Kill Ovid! I command You!

Part Four

Ovid is dying, thanks to You. Our protagonist is finally hanging from a cross, moaning pitifully. I am so proud of this—what would You call it?—hmmmm … if Christ's birth is a nativity, I'll just call this a *mortivity*—this mortivity. It is an opportunity to show how profound is my natural capacity for sympathy. Look at how forgivingly I cry for Ovid! Look at how lovingly I put my hand upon my bosom, furrow my brow, and curl my bottom lip into a convincing frown. Don't *You* just want a soul as full of compassion as this Author's?

OK, that's it for crocodilian crying. Ovid can fulfill his Christ-function in this story without our shining too bright a spotlight on him.

Though, now that this spotlight *is* upon Ovid, I look upon his ridiculous form, clad in only a loincloth.

Christ, Ovid is fat! It looks as though Buddha took a wrong turn and found his way into a Biblical illustration. I am starting to think that two nails won't do it. I might borrow a forklift just to support his paunch, which sags down from his torso, as full as a Kangaroo's pouch.

Ovid is making so many awful sounds—gurgling blood, throat rattling, gasping for air—it is as loud and startling as a manual-shift car without a clutch, about to stall. *Put-put-put-put ... plllfft.* I was right to prolong it. This is what I was waiting for. It is so much fun!

Sigh. This too shall pass.

☾

What is this, now?

A Man in a Black Coat walks up to Ovid, casting off his cloak. Paco is riding piggyback on Cain again! Paco climbs upon Ovid's cross and unbinds him. In a swift motion, Paco unplugs Ovid's hands and pulls him down. Is Paco Ovid's Sancho Panza now? And is Cain Ovid's ass?

What is going on?

My crucifixion plan is going all wrong!

Don't You worry, though; it's not Your fault. Paco, whom I'd always thought of as my most loyal avatar, is taking Ovid down from his cross, saving him in his dying hour. *Oh Paco, why art thou taking a stand against thy Author?*

Must I author two books now: for Paco and Cain, too? Must I concoct a list of bad guys for You to hunt down in *Roundabout Two: Out for Blood?* Must our killing-Ovid story turn into a

Rambo trilogy?

Down from his cross, Ovid is fading fast, losing blood from his stigmata. His pallor turns ghostly as blood is drawn away from his facial skin. Pools of blood form in his palms and, all along his body, spots of crimson show just how much Ovid's blood wants *out* of his body. His blood, following gravity's pull, down to his crotch, is causing Ovid's prick to stand upright. His bulky dick is poking out, pushing away his loincloth as though his body wants a last shot at copulation.

Anybody want to assist Ovid? Anybody? I didn't think so!

Ovid's humiliation is almost as fun as his dying! You and I and Abraham Lincoln stand around laughing. Ovid's big ugly dick is waving around, as though to say, "Hi, guys! I'm still working! I told you so!" with a Cyclops' wink. What a funny phallus! Ovid's shlong should find work as a stand-up comic.

Calling a taxicab, Paco hauls Ovid to a Cuban airport, puts Ovid on a flight to Chicago, lifts his body onto a train bound for Wisconsin, and brings him at last back to an OuLiPoCorp hospital in Madison.

All throughout this, You simply watch. And in watching, You allow it all to pass. How could You?

First Ovid, and Cain, and Paco, and now You, too? What kind of conspiracy is this, that Ovid turns against his Author, and Cain and Paco follow suit, and now *You* too simply watch as Ovid is brought to a hospital? Why don't You stop him? Why don't You do anything?

And You, Brutus?

As always, it is down to this: I am on my own. Killing Ovid is *my* duty. I cannot pass it on. I cannot pawn it off. It is not a hot potato, or musical chairs, or a round robin that can switch hands, from man to man, until I diminish my culpability down to nothing.

If I want to kill Ovid, I must do it with my own hands: by writing. Why is it so hard? What is blocking my way?

I try to kill him, and a curious thing always stays my hand.

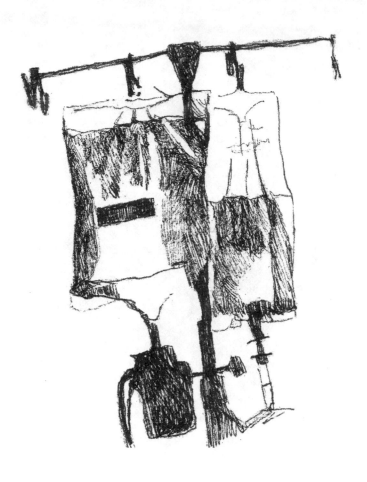

Fifth Part

Ovid is living, though his condition is critical. Our protagonist is in a coma, awaiting a blood transfusion from a willing donor. And who among us is willing to grant Ovid his blood?

Just as I thought. Nobody. Not You, not I, not anybody. To spill a drop of our own blood—a pinprick of pain—for a fictional individual such as Ovid is a ludicrous proposition. I would kill Ovid if I could. But it isn't working.

It's Murphy's Law in action: "Anything that *can* go wrong *will* go wrong."

My only consolation is that now Ovid is dying slowly. Watch: A doctor plugs him into a monitor; a woman in scrubs lifts him up and starts wiping his bottom; a bunch of doctors-in-training walk through his room and start taking notations. His mind is failing, and his body is not his own. Unlatching his skull, Ovid's Doctor is poking around, cutting apart, and now taking out half of his brain! If Ovid will not hang, Ovid is still losing his mind.

If only Ovid could stay conscious for this! If only Ovid could look at us now, watching him slowly fading away in his hospital gown, maintaining a vigil as though praying for his survival (but in fact praying for him to succumb to his doom). In living form, Ovid was always trying to avoid his Author's scrutiny. Now Ovid's *only* activity is to sit and allow his body to attract light, and absorb sight. Ovid is just an ontological fact, and not a full man. *Anata*, as Buddha says: "No soul."

I almost want to stir Ovid, waking him up with a "Ha-ha, I told you so. Na-na- na-na boo-boo!" It's such a vacant victory, without Ovid knowing of his loss. All this work I put into un-manning him, which I am now about to fulfill, and who is around to watch it? You? But I don't *know* You. I'm sorry, but I don't. You and I had our fun, and I thank You for Your collaboration, but it is no consolation for having Ovid numb to his own undoing.

You had a function in this: You sat in on our mock trial and You took my guilt away, validating my most maniacal and absurd fantasy by Your compliant will. But anybody could do what You did, starting from this book's first word and scanning it through to its last. I could pick up any two-bit scholar with an arts major who could do that, too, and I'd probably scam a composition or two out of him—full of flashy Franco-criticism—just as a bonus.

If You thought at first I was too hasty for Ovid's fall, now that it is within my grasp, I am lost in anticipation. I must fast-forward to find out what kills Ovid. His Author? Naturally, but how do I do it? What malicious plot spouts forth from my conniving brain now? I must know. So I must fast-forward.

Fast-forward ....

Whilst You and I wait, how about I bring back Cain? And Padlock? And OuLiPo, and Ovid's family, and our cast of thirty-six actors playing various officials, doctors, and ghosts? Look! All of us sit around now watching Ovid rot! It's station Ovid. Or a Broadway musical, playing out for a sold-out crowd of tourists. A spotlight on Ovid. His now-graying hair, his now-wrinkling skin. His now-grown-out hair, his now-flaking skin. His now-knotting hair, his now-drooping skin.

A hush falls on this crowd. Ovid's solo is approaching. Though isn't Ovid's song always a solo? But this is a solo of no sound. A *Waiting for Godot* for nitwits.

Fast-forward ....

Ovid will start to spasm, at first, vomiting up blood (for Ovid cannot swallow any food). *Huach! Huach!* Ah, what music! Gnashing his incisors, Ovid's fillings will pop out. *Clink, clink.* His tooth chips, and Ovid starts choking on a bit of his own tooth. *Kkhhh! Kkhhh! Hum-di-di-dum, da-da!*

Fast-forward ....

Finally, Ovid stirs, his digits tapping, his lids popping up, his body waking to its own dismal situation. Look at this: Ovid is conscious again! At last, Ovid knows that I won! But now I must act fast to finish him off.

Quick, bring in a doctor who forgot his Hippocratic oath ("First, do no wrong")! Find a young M.D. who will not shy away from killing a living thing—a doctor of "Youth in Asia." (And why is it, anyhow, that any doctor who works on youths in Asia is, according to this unusual word, automatically unscrupulous about killing? Pol Pot, Lon Nol, Norodom Sihanouk, doctors all! Surgical doctors slicing organs from an ailing Cambodia, a nation caught in a bloody civil war. That palindromic occultist Lon Nol! That psychotic madman Pol Pot! That crafty political accommodationist Sihanouk! What a cast of lunatics fit for a fiction. And proctoring this country's damnation is our own Dr. Richard Nixon—doom's right-hand man—a youth-in-Asia doctor midwifing a barbarous utopia. A holocaust. But it is just a word. Holocaust. But it is just a word.)

As I am musing on this distracting soliloquy, Ovid finds a way out! To my horror, Ovid unplugs his monitors, his IV, all his tubing and wiring and scanning apparati. Ovid jumps up from his hospital futon and, in a brilliant flash of godly light, slams arms-first into his hospital window, smashing glass and now squirting blood and hurling his body down and now falling, falling, falling, falling, falling—oh, it lasts for so long!—falling, falling, falling to a final *splat!*

No! Not this way! A suicidal Ovid is not what I fought so hard for! My glory, my Ovid, lost.

Undo! Go backwards! Alas, an hour, a day, a month, is an unforgiving thing. Now all I can do is mourn my own anticlimax. Now, all I can do is fast-forward.

Fast-forward ....

Part Six

Ovid's burial is not as jovial an occasion as it was in my imagination. Not all within this crowd of OuLiPoans has shown up to gloat, as I did, but many actually *mourn* his passing! Around us, a lot of sobbing, and blubbing, and acting foolish in honor of a fool. Why is it? Is it just that anybody at a public burial is automatically thinking about his own mortality? Or is all this crying and moaning truly out of pity for Ovid?

As it turns out, Ovid's story has actually brought about a cult following, his own quasi-spiritual tradition—a Manson family clan or a Branch Davidian spinoff. According to Abraham Lincoln, a nosy OuLiPoan got word of Ovid taking flight from his Author, and landing in a no-man's-land in which his Author cannot roam, and told his buddy, who told his buddy, and so on. And that is how so many mistook Ovid for a god.

Don't you fools know that I am God? Not Ovid!

Rows and rows of Ovid's faithful fill this squat, brick

building—an anonymous suburban church in Madison, Wisconsin—Ovid's old stomping grounds, and soon, ironically, his burial grounds. Paco—a loyal Ovidian (but a disloyal Authorian)—is staring into his shaking hands, at his twitching digits, as though adding up his guilt. Cain and Padlock both sit placidly and aloof, as though taking part in a stoicism showdown. Alyssa is crying out loud, in a public display of agony, to my dismay, so that I must walk out on Ovid and abandon this ridiculous ritual, taking in a bit of outdoor air. Away from it all, I am watching a last ray of daylight fall upon this church.

I do not wish to watch Alyssa mourning such a villain as Ovid. Alyssa is so charitably sorrowful that his bawling is contagious: All around Alyssa, Ovid's faithful cry out, too: raging, *raging*, against a dying of a light.

A sundown glow fills Madison: its clouds, its woods, its buildings.

Not far away, Harry Math is approaching, with Polly and Fozzy in tow. Not far away, following Harry Math and his Math family is Anzora, and Anzora's two kids.

What audacity, for Harry and Anzora to show up at Ovid's burial! Harry, Polly, Fozzy, Anzora, Frank, and Lana all sit down, unassumingly, in a back row of this church, as though not at all party to Ovid's downfall.

At last, a group of rational humans, who know that Ovid was, throughout it all, just a lousy good-for-nothing!

But what about Aaron? Scan this crowd on Your own. Can You find Aaron (or, failing that, can You find Waldo)?

Look all You want. Aaron is not amidst this crowd. What is Aaron doing that is so important that it took him away from his dad's burial?

Aaron is writing. Aaron is starting his own cult.

But look at this: Paco is raising a glass in honor of Ovid. Though I must say that raising up his arm only puts him on a horizontal stratum that is still a foot short of a normal man. It is Paco, oddly, who is toasting Ovid on this occasion.

"I didn't actually know Ovid until 2004, at a Holiday Inn in Arkansas. Ovid was running away, high on marijuana, and totally paranoid, thinking I was a munchkin from *Wizard of Oz*. But if I think about Ovid now, I don't think about all of that stuff. I think about what Ovid *said* that day: Humankind is looking for a quiddity. A quiddity of living as a thinking animal. It's a common thought, I know, but how many of us actually go out and *look* for it, as Ovid did?

"I do know this about him: Ovid is an organ donor, and all of his practical parts will go to any thankful man or woman lacking a lung or a diaphragm. So Ovid wasn't all that bad. Thank you." Clapping follows, with a handful of "Awwws" thrown in, upon watching Paco sip a bit of Pinot Noir from his tiny cup. Row by row, this crowd stands up in honor of Ovid.

Do not for an instant allow Paco to turn Ovid into a Saint. What kind of Roman Catholic would put forward *this man* for canonization, anyway?

Oh, no. Paco is not a Roman Catholic at all! Paco is in Ovid's cult! That is why Paco brought him down from his cross. But if Ovid is Paco's God, why didn't Paco allow You to crucify him, as a sacrificial lamb? Hmmm …. Ovid's faith must call for an anti-martyr—a god who is not *dying*, but *living*, for your sins. A survivor God, and not a sacrificial God.

Alyssa stands, honoring Ovid. Cain stands, too, and Corporal Padlock. Harry stands, and Anzora, and Li Po, too. Don't You stand, though. Your work with Ovid is not through.

You must bury Ovid. You must bury him. Don't stop at a standard, six-foot pit, but dig on and on until you must physically stop. But don't stop. Continuing to dig, through rock, through crust, through magma, past coal mining plants, past Doctor Von Hardwigg, burrow through all obstruction and difficulty, straining Your body to its limit.

Dig to China if you can! Turn Ovid Asian! Hand him a pair of chopsticks, stick a conical hat on him, and voilà! Instant Chinaman! (Or so says Hollywood, anyway.)

As long as Ovid is out of Our way.

Ovid—his rotting body, void of soul—is Asia's albatross now!

BOOK SIX

First Part

Follow Ovid. Past his physical paralysis. Past his coma, his partial lobotomy, his suicidal drop from a hospital window. Into purgatory.

Find Ovid in a waiting station, just as vast and drab as in Purgatorio. It is full of lost souls, not all-good, not all-bad, but spirits of a middling sort, many of whom did what Durand Durand and Ovid did—jump off of a tall building, or bail out of a flying airship—a train of spirits, just going on and on, a long wormy coil that spans from infinity to infinity.

In purgatory, day and night blur. All is gray, but soft, with low saturation and hardly any contrast, as though a haphazard artist took a normal day and did a touch-up on Photoshop using a "blur" tool. It looks, in fact, as thin and wispy as any painting that adorns OuLiPoCorp building's walls, in which artificial illuminations furnish a spot of color on a drab, rustic canvas.

You cannot say what color purgatory's sky is. On occasion, You will start to think about what sky-color it has, but cannot confirm it, as You find that You cannot go outdoors, but must stay in this room with no windows or doors. Soon You will abandon this thought, and sit down, robot-fashion, to watch TV.

Who is in purgatory with You and Ovid? It is full of agnostics, still doubting. It is full of ambiguity and vacillation. Afflicting all is a total lack of conviction (or a lack of trust in an all-knowing God-Author, as I am). In fact, it is full of practicing Christians, and Muslims; it has Buddhists, Hindus, Sikhs, Taoists, Wiccans, Spiritualists, and folks of all sorts of faiths and backgrounds (am I missing anybody?).

Ovid will look at his surrounding company. Konstantinos is in purgatory. Raymond Q is in purgatory. But what of Durand Durand? Ovid will walk around asking, "Do you know how I can find Durand Durand? Do you know him?"

And what of Anna? Was Anna brought up in a halo of light to God's domain, or thrown down into Satan's pit? Or is Anna just a ghost, an orphan immortal inhabiting a mortal world? Ovid cannot say what Anna is. But Anna is not in purgatory.

Thinking on this possibility—of an infinity without Anna, and still in thrall to his Author—Ovid will cry out, succumbing at last to that horror which I had long sought to draw out of him. But it is a dull joy, watching Ovid pull out his hair, fistful by fistful, wringing his hands. By dying in his own way, Ovid has shown how strong his will is, and my ability to control him is now always in doubt.

Though Ovid's pain is a kind of balm to my wounds.

Hark! Who is it that howls out in agony? Ovid! In purgatory! And nobody pays him any mind. Nobody in purgatory has any sympathy in surplus for a poor, sorrowing nobody. What did Ovid think? That Virgil would stand by awaiting his arrival? Or that Charon would boat him across Styx, his own individual conductor through purgatory?

Ha!

"What's so funny?" You might ask.

What's funny is that Ovid thinks that dying is his final salvation, his triumphant flight from his Author! It is not so. Right now, Ovid is in purgatory—God's waiting station. But if Ovid winds up in God's own domain, Ovid will find that I am God. And if Ovid spirals down into Satan's pit, Ovid will find that I am Satan, too. And as Satan's minions claw at his innards and swallow his organs, causing pain such as only a soul in damnation can know, Ovid will look down and catch his first look at his Author.

Hi, Ovid! This too shall pass!

Isn't it a curious consolation, that a fictional man's conscious mind can outlast his body, but not so with us? It's a conundrum You and I put up with, day in and day out—that our own story's conclusion is shut off from us, not knowing if a postscript is a distant possibility. A fictional individual is lucky: for him, dying is not such a tragic thing; a work of fiction is not living to start with. Paradoxically, it is Ovid who cannot pass away, though I stop writing, though You put down this book, though I kill him in a thousand ways. So Ovid must submit to pain and sorrow and humiliation. That is what it costs, immortality.

Thus Anna is shut off from him for good, and I will finally show You how. I am bringing Anna up into my glorious domain, and no soul will gain admission into this nirvana but us. I am building a happy hunting ground (in which only I hunt, and in which Anna is my only quarry), and I act with Anna as God acts towards His faithful in that Biblical Book of Amos: which is to say, I control Anna, consort with Anna, subduing this good woman—a suburban hausfrau—spoiling Ovid's bounty. "You look familiar," says Anna, laying out on my God-sofa.

"So do you," I say, playing along. "Do you always hang out at this bar?"

"Not at all. This is my first," says fantasy-Anna.

"Your first, you say? Was your son a virgin birth?" I want to

231

know. By focusing on Ovid, was I looking for a Christ-symbol in a wrong Dullann? Is it Aaron who is actually a son-of-a-God? I think so!

I tactfully put out a "Do Not Disturb" sign on our door. Shutting our blinds, I turn around and start "tickling Anna's foot." And my, oh my, is our Anna ticklish.

So now You know. Ovid is put away in soul prison, and Anna is my trophy, my post-storm rainbow. All of this—my plotting, my roundabout way of killing off my protagonist, my show-boating and acting all big for my sadistic public—is in its final appraisal, just a classic romantic yarn about an Author who courts a girl: his own protagonist's woman. My authorship, as it turns out, is just a cloak for an amorous inclination.

Anna, my brainchild. My fantasy woman. My pillow-book.

You do not know how I did long for Anna throughout this story, how I did lust for only a touch. But physical contact with a fictional woman is illusory; it is only a product of our imagination. Which is why Anzora had to kill Anna—to turn Anna into a ghost, to join us Gods and Authors in our abyss. Oh, I know that romantics say that souls bond in an immortal hand-clasp, as though man and woman could stroll in Paris for all infinity. But this Author wants only to ravish Anna, our fictional protagonist's fictional lady, in most graphic and pornographic ways.

Alas, I am but an Author; and Anna is but an Author's spawn. But, I can ravish Anna with words, cunnilinguistically. And You can watch. And nobody in Your world can do anything, for Anna is fictional, and as Ovid's jury has shown (including You, its sixth jurist), fictional individuals do not count for squat in affairs of human rights.

I start off with a bit of gratuitous sado-masochism. Whips, chains, cock-rings, butt-plugs, strap-on dildos, vibrators, handcuffs, blindfolds, ball-gags, a suit of armor, tight plastic pants, shiny black boots. Rockstar stuff.

I sing Anna's body digital. I sing, I sing....

And if you start to doubt my sanity—if you ask, "Is this a parody? Has our Author totally lost his mind, which is now full of only sick illusions and fantasy?"— I will simply say, as Portnoy did: "Who? Whom am I harming with my lusts?"

Part Two

Purgatory's only art-form is sitcom. Purgatorians watch sitcoms, and inhabit sitcoms that purgatorians, in turn, will watch. A TV show in which a TV cast will watch TV on TV. It is a circular world, always looping in on its point of origin, an infinity of duplication: an Ouroboros, swallowing its own tail, growing to gargantuan proportion, from a worm into an anaconda, and finally surrounding this world—always consuming, always growing, until Ragnarok's arrival....

Living in a TV studio is at first discomfiting, but it grows on You (slowly, as a fungus grows on a lump of shit).

In a too-bright living room that allows no shadows at all, Ovid is sitting on a couch watching TV with his sitcom family. His "family" is a cast that consists of a woman of thirty—a tad too young for Ovid—and a brood of six kids: two natural births, two in vitro, and two adoptions—from Africa *and* Asia!—all boys). Smart, snappy dialog spills from this group as though it is normal for a family to talk with such casual aplomb.

"This plasma TV is rad, Dad!" his first son shouts out. "It's all automatic," says Ovid, showing off all its plug-ins.

"What was wrong with our old LCD?" asks Ovid's young arm-trophy in a shrill nasal twang.

"Bah, you girls! You wouldn't know anything about it. It's a guy thing." Ovid looks to his sons, who all laugh along with him. A laugh track joins in. "And don't worry… it's a Sony!" Ovid adds. Sony is a sponsor for Ovid's show.

"It's all HD now, Ma," says son two. "That LCD stuff is so 2004."

"I must admit, it has an uncanny similarity to how things actually look. It's as though I'm looking out of our living-room window!" says his mom.

"C'mon! You wouldn't find that kind of girl out of our living-room window… not in this town," says Ovid, nudging his son's ribs. A laugh track again. Is it laughing with Ovid, or at him?

"That visual and audio quality is so good on our TV, now I gotta go out and buy a Blu-Ray!" says his third son.

"Don't worry!" says Ovid, and all his sons say it with him in unison: "It's a Sony!"

In an ordinary sitcom, this is that point at which you might start to think, "I'll just flip to HSN," and Your kids will say, "Mom, Dad, I want to watch cartoons!" At which point Your own family drama will start up. But not so in purgatory. In this particular world, this sitcom is ongoing, and You cannot turn it off.

"What's for lunch, Dad?" asks his sixth and last son.

"I don't know about You, but I'm having a Big Mac™!" says Ovid. McDonald's is also a sponsor.

A chorus of "Hooray!" and "Yahoo!" pours out, and a tray of junk food magically pops up. Ovid's kids dig in, as happy as pigs at a trough.

Soon, a quasi-plot forms. First son is caught shoplifting, and brought back in a cop car. With faux contrition, First Son says,

"I'm sorry. I'm so, so sorry," again and again. It is this cyclical apology that such sitcoms condition all purgatorians to mimic. Upon watching Ovid's show, purgatorians walk around all day saying, "I'm sorry. I'm so, so sorry," without knowing why.

In punishing his wayward son, Ovid must maintain a cool, diplomatic quality, whilst also putting on a patriarchal air. It is a balancing act. It is Daddy training, Bill Cosby fashion (with all its accompanying hypocrisy). But why? Purgatorians cannot spawn, nor grow up, nor grow old. A purgatorian family is a sitcom family, cast with only this goal in mind: quirky dialog, with occasional schmaltz. It is simply going through so many motions, punishing his son (but lovingly so!), almost as proof that a cosmic disciplinary God is watching.

But Ovid's family is, ironically, ignoring this fact: that First Son's habit for shoplifting is only a byproduct of his family's morality, as natural as a bird taking worms from its mama. Buying things is Ovid's only occupation in this world, so it is with his sons. This pit was dug by Ovid, toy by toy, fashion by fashion, gizmo by gizmo. And now it is burying him.

Don't worry, Ovid. This too shall pass.

In this half-hour program, laughing is not a sign of joy, but a compulsion, as though a jackal is living within us. Or laughing gas is pouring out from an air duct. It is painful, laughing in this way—I am dying laughing!—so a laugh track must pick up our slack.

Now You walk in, stumbling as You do, and falling in front of Ovid. A laugh track follows. Hilarity! Ovid grouchily complains that Your body is blocking his plasma TV. You try to roll away, but your foot is stuck! Ovid picks up a pillow and throws it at You. You duck. Ovid throws a can of Pabst™ at You, and a McDonald's Big Mac™, and a bag of Doritos™ (sponsors all!). Ovid throws tools, plant stands, chairs, all his suburban comforts—his bowl of plastic fruit. Missing You, a stray banana hits an old woman standing in this studio's front row.

"Ooooh," says this crowd, provokingly.

Ovid is too unfunny, his antics too pat and obvious. His studio is full of purgatorians, who start to throw Ovid's fruit back at him. Ovid cannot catch anything (his past association with sports is a tragic history of kids picking him last, and having his daily badminton training cut short by a stray football knocking him unconscious), so Ovid just falls down and rolls into a ditch. As Ovid looks up, handfuls of fruit fly past him.

Who forgot to turn off this show's laugh track? Why is it still going on, as Ovid is struck by a guava, a papaya—how odd to throw tropical fruit!—and a stray tomato (a tomato is not culinarily a fruit, but botanically, it is) hits You on Your arm, ruining Your suit coat?

As this food fight winnows down to its last two combatants, both of whom quickly burn out, and slink off, soon it is down to Ovid and his old fruit. Its odor draws a swarm of bugs, among which is that glorious biological curiosity: Drosophila. A fruit fly! (But I could wax rhapsodic about Drosophila until I run out of ink, so I will withhold my fruit-fly fanaticism.)

Now who is this, walking into our studio, into all this spoliation and ruin? It is not a fruit fly, nor Ovid's sitcom family, or any purgatorian at all. It is Aaron, son of Ovid (his actual son, from his own loins, and not a sitcom child, acting it out for pay), holding aloft a bag. But what is in his bag? Is it a MacGuffin? A McMuffin™?

Ovid thinks, "Is Aaron following in my path now, to purgatory, to oblivion?" In this studio's background, Ovid's sitcom song plays on constant loop, turn-tabling, around and around as a whirligig in a gust of wind: "Old MacDonald had a farm… I… I… O!"

℃

Aaron stands upright amidst this chaos of shifting things, walking through an inch-high pool of fruit guts, lifting Ovid up to a sitting position and crouching down on his right, stabilizing him. Ovid looks upon Aaron with a sublimity that is worthy of a mad king, staring into a vision of Banquo's ghost. (Didn't I say, in Book Two, that Ovid's was simply a story "told by an idiot, full of sound and fury, signifying nothing"?)

"Aaron! Did our Author put you in purgatory too?" Ovid asks. "Did I kill you, as I am said to kill all my family?"

"But Ovid, this is not purgatory," Aaron says, cryptically. "Or if it is, it is only a purgatory of your own making."

Ovid, still hazy from his attack, sits staring at his son, his thoughts moving in slow motion. Circling his mind, as birds whirl around a mound of carrion, is this word: "Tomorrow." Tomorrow and Tomorrow and Tomorrow.... Why is Ovid constantly thinking about Tomorrow, our fifth jurist?

"What is this world that I'm in?" Ovid asks. "Is this still Guantanamo? Or is it a grand prank, a *Truman Show* or *Matrix* world, built just for yours truly?"

Aaron lifts Ovid onto a barstool. Ovid is still portly, and balding, stubbly from months without a razor. Aaron is slight, but compact, with dark hair and an unnaturally adult quality that looks disturbing if staring out from a child, as it is with Aaron. "Right now, Ovid, you simply inhabit your own mind, moving from gland to gland, passing from blood to brain and back again," Aaron says.

"So I am still living? This isn't a posthumous world at all?" Ovid asks.

"As much as you can call it living," Aaron says. Ovid nods, thinking what a dismal thing it is to imprison a man's mind within a sitcom plot. "But is it truly living, if you must go on living without Christ?"

"Christ! Who said anything about Christ?" Ovid is trying to stand up, almost functional now, with a look of slow horror dawning on him.

"Christ! Our Lord and Savior!" Aaron shouts, in bliss (or in illusory bliss).

"Oh, no. Not my son!" Ovid sits back down.

"But I am just a child of God," Aaron says.

"No! No! It is my child standing in front of my vacant soul right now. Not God's! My son! Not God's!" This is Ovid at his most furious.

"You cannot own a man. That is, not a man of God," Aaron says, with platitudinous calm.

Ovid, sizing up Aaron 2.0 and his blank robotic look, thinks, "This is not a 'Man of God.' This is a 'Man-o'-War,' a squiddish monstrosity fit for scraping along Atlantic's bottom."

"That is why I am visiting You," Aaron says, "to bring you God's word…"

"I don't want God's words, Aaron. And I don't want my Author's words. I want your words, Aaron. Talk to your Dad. Talk to Ovid! Don't just transmit Biblical truisms, or spout Christian aphorisms." Ovid is practically clawing at his hair now (or what bit of hair still adorns his balding crown). "I know that I was a bad Daddy to you—always busy with a book, or a song, or a painting, with no thought for my own child. And I know that my abandoning you was giving up on our family, sacrificing my authority as your Dad. But do not turn into an automaton. Do not throw away this gift of individuality."

"I am not throwing anything away," Aaron says, "I am giving you a gift. Your body has had a burial, but your blood is still flowing in your body, and your brain is still functioning."

"So I am living, but in a coffin?" Ovid asks. "What am I? A blood-sucking ghoul? A vampiric spirit?"

"No, and no. This," Aaron says, making a motion with his arm that contains all his surroundings, "is your mind. In your thoughts, a fraction of an instant might last for days, or months. Your synaptic world can go on and on, though your physical body is dying."

"So, supposing I can bust out of this thought-prison, and my body stirs up, and I am conscious again— will I simply wind up dying by suffocation anyway?"

Aaron nods darkly.

"If that's what's going on, I am staying in purgatory, for good," Ovid says, with conviction. "It is my only skill: to truck through day by day in a world of doldrums, without complaint. That is how I got by working at OuLiPoCorp, and that is how I will avoid dying in purgatory. Monotony is my playground now."

"But didn't God grant you this stay with a goal in mind? Don't you think God has a grand plan?" Aaron says.

"My Author has a grand plan, and that is for Ovid to hang upon a cross, as a Christ-symbol, dying for your sins. But I am not a martyr! I will not go willingly into that trap again." Raising his fist, Ovid scowls up at his Author (though "up," "down," "backwards," and "forwards" imply nothing in a world of total imagination, such as Ovid inhabits now).

"Don't you think," Aaron says, "that your function in this halfway world is to look for salvation, and that this prolongation of your survival is to a point: that you might find God?"

"Find God?" Ovid says, fortifying his spirit and finally standing up on his own. "Is God lost? Is God a navigator of a ship, with a compass and a chart, trying to find his way through a storm? Is God a tourist, with a map and a backpack, looking for famous buildings and fountains and things to photograph and put in his scrapbook?"

Ovid grows dizzy, and sits back down again. Lights blur all about him, but Ovid stays conscious, though faintly.

Aaron clasps Ovid's hand again and says, "Don't you want to attain God's gift? To go, finally, to that immortal land that awaits any just and faithful man?"

"But I am unjust. And I am unfaithful. And I am guilty, guilty, guilty!" Ovid cannot contain his sorrow. His chin falls into his palms, and his ocular ducts pour forth as though salivating, Pavlovian-fashion, upon sight of a lamb shank.

I cannot stand to watch Ovid hand-wringing and blabbing on about his guilt. I don't know if I want to snuff him out or to bring him back for round two.

But Ovid is dying, trying to wrap his brain around this fact, but cannot. Can any man harbor a vision of a world without him in it? Could You construct, with all Your vast capacity of imagination, a continuous world, past that in which You walk and talk and sit and shit and want and want and want? It is upon this truth that Ovid thinks, and upon which I think, and upon which You think.

What is a world, without You? And what kind of a world is within You? A world without. A world within.

In... Out... In... Out...

Third Part

In his thoughts, Ovid is his own Author. And now that Ovid inhabits a world of total thought, Ovid is finally in control, though Ovid may not know it. Nothing short of this—not king, nor ghost, nor god—could contradict my command. (As You know by now, no man who is born of woman can vanquish this Author!) It is only in his corrupt imagination that Ovid is truly autonomous, truly individual. Ovid has control, but in accommodating his ways to my dominion for so long, Ovid hardly knows what to do with it.

So Ovid and Aaron, with no longstanding family traditions, and with nothing at all in common, sit down and watch TV, as purgatorians always do. A gap that could fit two grown adults sits in that saggy spot twixt Aaron and Ovid, on this couch—that spot into which, ordinarily, a happily bonding Dad and Son would fit.

But on TV, Ovid spots a familiar sight: Durand Durand! If this isn't purgatory, it is a fair approximation of it, as it contains a man who is known to inhabit Limbo (which is only two doors down from purgatory). On TV, Durand Durand is a star. His is a sort of Quiz Show (that a Christian purgatorian thought of titling, with no hint of irony, *Noah's Ark*), in which smart guys go man-to-man in random trivia on topics ranging from Babylonian history to pop music, and naturally, in this world, Durand Durand is dominant: an alpha dog of factoids and arcana.

On Durand Durand's program, though, playing "trivia" is akin to war. Its winning combatant will sail off on Noah's Ark, and his rivals will all drown in a flood.

Upon drowning, his rivals will swirl downward in a big flush, as turds do in a lavatory stall.

Now, as Ovid is still privy to his subconscious mind's whim, his surroundings transform involuntarily: Ovid and Aaron now stand at opposing podiums in a studio, scoring boards all alight. Durand Durand is running this show, holding a mic to his lips and giving his introductory talk on "How to Play Noah's Ark":

"First, Ovid will put an inquiry to Aaron, and Aaron to Ovid. Both must furnish a word or two clarifying that point to my satisfaction—but only a word or two—as a sort of ongoing FAQ, back and forth as a ping-pong ball by a pair of Asian Olympians, until party 'A' or party 'B'"— or party "O," for Ovid—"is dumbfound."

Ah, but I found Ovid dumb upon his birth, on April Fool's Day.

"At that point, this Quiz Show's winning party must clarify a last point, and failing that, both Ovid and Aaron will drown in a flood. On such an occasion, Noah's Ark is simply an animal transport ship with nobody to captain it: a boat afloat on a vast, dark flood."

First Round

Ovid starts. "Um... What is Japan's capital city?" Ovid says, struggling to think of anything particularly difficult to ask.

"Tokyo," Aaron says, quickly. "Why did you abandon us?" Aaron throws out. Ovid turns towards Durand Durand—this show's arbitrator—to assist him, but Durand Durand won't butt in.

"Paranoia," Ovid finally puts forward. And that is all. Only a word.

Round Two

Ovid still finds it hard to bring a random thought to mind, out of nothing. "Uh... what is an Aardvark's food?"

"Ants," Aaron says, just as quickly. And Ovid thinks, "Good going, son! Aaron is such a smart kid! And so good at this trivia stuff.... But if I allow him to win, I will drown in a swamp of filth!"

Aaron, pointing at Ovid, asks, "What is worth dying for? Family? Country? God?"

"No abstraction is worth dying for," Ovid says, "including loyalty." Buzzzz.

Durand Durand shuts off Ovid's mic, who is flouting quiz show law by failing to stick to his two-word limit.

Third Round

"How did you find your way into purgatory?" Ovid asks Aaron.

"By writing," Aaron says, cryptically. As soon as this word is out, it brings about an abrupt halt in Aaron and Ovid's colloquial flow, as though a cosmic functionary has put our continuum on hold just so that Aaron and Ovid could savor a slow inhalation of air. Whilst on hold, smooth jazz plays continuously, blandly oozing its alto-sax rhythms, pouring out of a distant radio, crackling invisibly.

Ovid starts to think that Aaron is dumbfound, but Aaron finds his vocal ability. Finally, Aaron asks, "What kind of a man is Ovid?"

Ovid will slump down a bit, looking downcast, a casualty of too much truth. "An addict."

"What kind of an addict?" Aaron says. Buzzzz. Aaron is running afoul of quiz show law by posing a follow-up to his first inquiry.

Round Four

Thinking uncomfortably long, Ovid says, "What school do you go to now?"

"Right now I am still in high school. But if, post-graduation, I am still stuck in your brain, I plan on matriculating into hippocampus." Buzzzz. Again, too much information. "If I go to school in your brain, will you pay my tuition?" Buzzz.

Ovid says, "Only if you major in accounting." Buzzzz.

"But I was thinking..." Buzzzz... "of studying..." Buzzzz... "spatial navigation," says Aaron. Buzzzz.

Fifth Round

"It's my turn," Ovid says, butting in. "What is in that bag of yours?" Ovid asks, pointing to Aaron's bulging knapsack.

"My book," Aaron says. "Do you truly plan on staying in purgatory?"

"I do," Ovid says.

Round Six

"What do you call this book?" Ovid asks, still curious about Aaron's bag.

"Null and Void," Aaron says, and looks as though Aaron is about to follow up with a clarification, but waits, drawing out Ovid's anticipation.

Afraid to ask, Ovid says, almost inaudibly, "And what is it about?" Buzzzz. His mouth is dry and sticky. His brain is buzzing. Buzzzz. Buzzzz.

"It's about you, Ovid," his son says. Buzzzz.

It is as though Ovid is hit with a club, stunning him into submission. Ovid is standing upright, but dizzily, a halo of

247

stars spinning around him: a cartoon Bluto with his lights out. Pacing now, his foot cannot find solid ground. Ovid trips, toppling into a railing, and his hands cling to it.

"How could you, Aaron?" Ovid thinks, but vocalizing anything at this point is difficult for him. His gut hurts, though Ovid has no body. Ovid's own soul is a wound.

It occurs to Ovid—clinging onto this railing, looking up at his son, grown tall and broad whilst Ovid was away—that, by abandoning Aaron, Ovid was not saving him from Darth Ovid at all. No, far from it, Ovid's son was now Darth Aaron, and just as it dawns upon him, that armor-clad villain is raising his fist in triumph.

"Ovid, I am your Author!" I say, with Aaron's mouth, in Aaron's skin, within which I was hiding all along.

Buzzzz.

"What do you think about that, Ovid?" I ask, gloating in my victory.

Ovid is struck dumb. That awful lack of sound. His horror vacui is flaring up; ignoring it is a virtual impossibility. Random words pop into Ovid's mind: Axon, glial, hypothalamus, divinity. "A man's mind is his God." Who said that? Who is talking into Ovid's brain? Ovid is trying to think!

"Look at you, Ovid," I say. "If you win at Noah's Ark, congratulations; you kill your own son!"

Again, that waiting "music" plays, smooth jazz on drums and sax, and Ovid holds his hands up to stop that sound, but it grows and builds, and turns into a blaring horn, a thumping rhythm, and finally, a busy signal.

Ovid is cut off in mid-dialog. Noah's Ark is rising.

Ovid shuts his lids tight, wrapping his body around his podium, constricting it with his arms, waiting for a flood. And as it starts to flood, to Ovid's alarm, it is not just him, but Aaron, You, and Durand Durand, too, caught up in this downpour.

It flows outward, at first, as though riding on a Gravitron at Six Flags, or a twirl-a-whirl spun too quickly by a fat kid at a playground. But it flows inward soon, and Ovid, Aaron, and Durand Durand, too, all spill down into what, it turns out, is not just a whirlpool, but a whirl-portal, transporting Ovid and his band of misfits into a sci-fi fantasy.

Part Four

I'm Aaron— so what? A sadistic kid with a magnifying glass, fond of burning things, with a playing-God fantasy and a killing-Ovid fixation? Who did you think it was? Col. Mustard in a billiards room with a cup of poison? Sorry, but this Whodunit is not so fraught with logical or psycho-logical intricacy.

Did I just kill my dad and ravish my mom in a blatant bid for psychological scrutiny? Oops!

But I am not Aaron Dullann of minor pranks and strip clubs; nor am I Aaron Dullann of Jacuzzi baptisms and Christian rock. I am Aaron 4.0 (my third incarnation as a Hari Krishna didn't work out). My cultish inclination is intact, naturally, but I am my own guru now. And my following is growing.

Will You join us? Will You aid in my mission to kill Ovid? Or is this patricidal and matriphilic story going too far?

"This is too much," You say? "I want out," You say?

OK, if You and I must part ways, it's only fair to split Ovid up, fifty-fifty. I will claim Ovid's soul, and You can lay claim to his body. Just dig him up and stuff him!

Within a day or two, I will mail You a thank-you card: "Thank you for participating in my assault on Ovid, for sitting on his jury, and damning him to purgatory. XOXO—Author." That tonal quality is just right for this awkward (dis)association of ours.

This distant-family back-and-forth of Ours puts You in a position of honorary cousin. Can I count You in for Thanksgiving? What if I allow You to bring Ovid along? I almost forgot! Ovid is just a carcass. But so what? Bring him anyway! It will add to our fun, to doll him up and lay him out on our porch, propping up his hand as though waving at boardwalk traffic. In a cozy cabin along California's coast, You will bury him up to his chin in sand. If Ovid attracts maggots, spray him with bug spray.

Look how handy Ovid is! Prop him up in Your car, riding shotgun, as if in a carpool, and watch how quickly you roll down California's highways. Bring him to lunch, and don't worry about looking pitiful, sitting in a booth all on your own. If you wind up short on cash, You can always find Ovid a job as a CPR dummy, or as a blow-up doll for an anatomy class, or as a crash victim on TV.

On TV, Ovid's body could attain stardom! Look at how many famous "actors" slip by our cultural radar and pull off a multi-million-dollar film, though so insubstantial and vapid that it is hard to say if such an "artist" contains as much soul as a cardboard cutout. Paris Hilton! Lindsay Lohan! Kim Kardashian! Ovid's rotting body would fit right in with this crowd of landfill-spawning carrion. Put a frilly shirt on him, and add a pair of transition bifocals. With just a pout of his lip (Botox), and an arch of his brow (Botox), this stiff could go off and sign a contract with a Hollywood studio for big bucks!

I want to watch Ovid go through his obligatory tabloid crisis, spiraling into drugs, shacking up with young girls of low morals, with paparazzi photographing all his folly, and bringing such dishonor, guilt, and opprobrium upon him that Ovid asks, "Is this all? Am I truly living, if I am living on display?"

It is particularly amusing for Ovid—as a cold, rotting body—to put forward such an inquiry. "Am I truly living?" No, Ovid, no!

Fifth Part

Ovid's thought-purgatory is starting to look pornographic:
all soft-glow and poorly lit. It is a hypnotic world of slow-
moving liquid, a volcanic magma churning as though from a
Jacuzzi, or as if Ovid is swimming in a lava lamp, and all of it
lit by a two-dollar black light. It is in fact Lythion, a sci-fi world
in which Matmos—a liquid that is a physical incarnation of
"bad psychic vibrations"—controls all within it. Having got rid
of his author, Ovid's imitation-god is just a vat of cosmic mud!
That is what I call a corrupt imagination!

But as soon as Ovid, You, I, and Durand Durand all touch
solid ground, things start to go wrong. Drowning in a flood
cannot stop Ovid's brain from manufacturing horror upon

horror to inflict on his own subconscious. Ovid's own mind turns against him, using anything within its grasp, starting with Durand Durand.

Durand Durand spirals into insanity, unstuck from his last strand of rationality. In Ovid's purgatory, Durand Durand is not just an OuLiPoan, not just a moody ghost with a habit for trivia, but a madman stockpiling WMDs: a "Positronic Ray" with which to bring about world-annihilation. Plus, a dooms-day bomb that nobody can stop—and nobody wants to: a bomb that kills with joy. This orgasm bomb throws us all into total chaos!

Ovid must stop Durand! That is why God is granting Ovid this stay—this is His grand plan—that Ovid should stop Durand Durand from fulfilling his world-annihilating ambi-tion. Crashing his ship on a moon orbiting Lythion, Ovid must instantly fight off a hoard of vicious, tooth-baring dolls. And that is not all.

On his way to stop Durand Durand, a group of horny guys mob Ovid, swash- buckling, trying to sword-fight him in mor-tal combat (using swords not of iron, but of skin). So many cocks block his way! It's as though Ovid is visiting a land of Moon-Amazons, though not from a high school fantasy, but from an LSD trip going horribly wrong, putting at risk Ovid's nocturnal mission.

Mark Hand puts his hands upon Ovid's thigh, and Ovid must cast it off. Dildano will try to touch his naughty parts, and Ovid will jump; Dildano will try to kiss him on his mouth, and Ovid will duck. It's as though Ovid is stuck in a porno Mario Bros.TM! And now Pygar, a blind man with wings, wants to join in! It's barbaric, or barbarian. Babar-ian? Barbara-ian?

Any way you cut it, Ovid is full of homophobic disgust. "No, I am not homophobic!" Ovid shouts out, against his Author's narration. "I am an old-school hippy, a Baby Boom kid! I couldn't possibly hold any homophobic notions in my notoriously broad and forward-looking mind."

Shut up! Daddy is writing. Sound familiar, Ovid?

Oddly, this attack by a mob of amorous guys brings about, in Ovid, a profound sympathy for womanhood: that, just to avoid having a man harass you day in and day out, a girl has to fight off attacks of this kind from high school straight through to adulthood.

"If I am homophobic, is it just a mask for my own inclinations?" Ovid asks. "Am I also a woman within (just as Alyssa is a man within)? How many guys or girls can an individual actually fit within him? Am I a Russian doll, a matryoshka? A man within a woman within a man within a woman within a man?

"No! I am not an onion!" Ovid shouts, pushing through this crowd, crashing through a wall of invisibility, into Durand Durand's "Vision Room."

Now Durand Durand has his hand on a shiny button, about to push down on it with his palm. "Wait, Ovid! Stand back! Or I will finish off your son, just by touching this button!"

Ovid cannot contain this thought: "Which son?" Growing angry, Ovid is about to attack. But staring at Durand Durand's amorphous form, it's as though Ovid is looking into a mirror: slightly off, a bit out-of-focus.

Ovid and Durand Durand: two mildly autistic agnostic insomniacs, gradually balding, midriff-bulging, socially awkward OuLiPians, adrift in an uncaring world. "Why didn't I jump with you?" Ovid asks Durand Durand, collapsing in front of him. "Why did I think that I was worthy of living, and not you?"

"You could not stop my fall. Just as you cannot stop your son's fall now." In slow motion, Durand Durand is pushing down on that fatal button. But Ovid jumps forward, knocking Durand Durand down, unplugging his Positronic Ray, standing proud and triumphant in his spot. Though just as Ovid is about to undo Durand Durand's joy-bomb, a shift in surroundings will occur, transporting him to Manhattan, during Cold-Warrior Ronald Ray-Gun's administration. Looking around, Ovid finds his surroundings oddly familiar:

This trio—Ovid, I, and Durand Durand—is standing atop a building, carrying Proton packs, confronting Zuul. Obviously, Durand Durand is cast as Harold Ramis. I, though just a child at that point, can pull off a fair imitation of Bill Murray. And Ovid, as Dan Akroyd, is busy trying to think of nothing, nothing at all. Any thought can bring about an apocalyptic conclusion. So Ovid must shut off his mind. But it won't work.

As a young man, Ovid would watch that film on a loop, again and again, studying its most insignificant dialog. For Ovid to inhabit Ray, and for him not to think of Stay Puft Marshmallow Man whilst doing so, is too much to ask.

Who You gonna call? Ghost Ovid!

As you know, a giant Stay Puft Marshmallow Man is about to stomp through this country's financial capital, crushing cars, toppling buildings, causing traffic jams, gridlock, and all kinds of chaos. Smiling throughout it all, Giant Stay Puft

Marshmallow Man is happily stomping upon that city's tourist industry, disturbing its calm, cool urbanity. Watch out for that hip thrift shop! Don't crush that stylish sushi bar!

A group of angry suits is lining up at city hall, filing so many complaints against him. It won't work. Giant Stay Puft Marshmallow Man is not a slum-lord, or a two-bit scam artist. Nor is his walk through downtown a publicity stunt, or a Macy's Day float. Accounts of paranormal activity go up and up, soaring (as a ghost soars—flowingly, ominously) past any known ghost story in history.

It's not just Anna, and Durand Durand, and that ghost-librarian now. It is a city of ghosts, and this many ghosts start to crowd out all of Manhattan's living population, who promptly go to Brooklyn.

Too many ghosts to ghost-bust! Although Ray (or Ovid, or Dan Akroyd) and his two pals cross rays, Zuul slips away to fight again tomorrow, and will not finish until Ovid's world is in thrall to his dominion.

Why must Ovid's imagination go on manufacturing horror upon horror? Why can't his lizard brain simply unclasp its slimy fist?

☾

Ovid's brain is a ShamWowTM, sopping up all of this stuff: random trivia, minor facts, crossword words, Sudoku shortcuts, books full of naval-gazing and willful obscurity, Cold War sci-fi films. And most of all, quotation upon quotation, with no thought to its background or origin. Quality is no commodity.

Which dinosaur, from a fossil found in Mongolia, is known for robbing roosts and absconding with ovum not his own? Oviraptor!

Talking of Mongolia: What would you call a shamanistic cairn, built out of rock or wood, that is symbolic of sky-worship in that country? An ovoo!

Putting away all this talk of rocks and wood, what do you call a study of glass compounds, which brought about CD's and DVD's? Ovonics!

Ovid's databank is full of Ovidian information, with no room for non-Ovidian facts. Ovid's naval-gazing is so all-consuming, Ovid will pick out lint from his dirty omphalos as though it is gold spun from straw. This duty is as important to Ovid as a holy ritual, tickling his nub as though it is a masturbatory act (though Ovid calls it art!).

What if Ovid wasn't born on April Fool's Day, in Mars' sky? What if his birthday was January first, and his astrological sign was Capricorn, in Saturn's month? Would Ovid's DNA contain a dash of humility?

What if? What if?

It is no good wracking our brains on this point: An Ovid is an Ovid is an Ovid. So many "what ifs" can only bring about a habit for dissatisfaction, and turn us all into Ovidians.

How many buttons fit into this jar? Roundabout a thousand?

How many days in a man's mortal duration? Roundabout thirty-thousand? How many options will Ovid shut off for good, idling in this masochistic fantasy? Roundabout a million?

No! Don't think about it! Look at what is occurring right now, as Ovid has lost control of his unconscious mind:

Hot hail is falling from Mongo. Our moon is out of orbit. Ming is manipulating clouds, causing tidal shifts, and bringing tsunamis, with a flick of his wrist and a push of a button. Ovid thought that Durand Durand and his Positronic Ray was bad! Ming is at fault for all of our global hardships! Ming is king, and Ming is trying to turn our world into a part of his Ming dynasty.

Ovid, as football star Flash Gordon, is shot out of a cannon into a dark, cold night. Dr. Zarkov (who looks suspiciously similar to Durand Durand, with his wild-looking hair and constant mumbling) and Flash Gordon land on Mongo, incognito.

Flash Ovidon and Dr. Durandkov wind up stumbling upon a party in honor of Ming. All his vassals stand in a row, carrying gifts with which to satisfy this notorious villain. It's a Ming Christmas! If a vassal hands him a gift that Ming wouldn't want, Ming lifts his hand, undoing him with a zap and a poof. "So, it is Ming's ring that controls this crowd," Flash Ovid thinks.

Among Ming's vassals Ovid spots his son Aaron— a Viking bird-man— as Vultan, a hawkman king. "Hail Ming!" I say, as Vultan, handing Ming a big chunk of crystal (which I took from a Robin-Hood-looking doofus known as "Barin," a royal Arborian). A fight bursts out, and amidst this clamor, Ming spots Flash Gordon and calls a halt to this impromptu combat.

I almost forgot: A random woman is accompanying Flash Gordon and Dr. Zarkov on this outing (I'll just call that woman "You"); and Ming, spotting You, thinks it is his gift from Flash Ovid and Durand Zarkov. Flash Gordon will try to stop him, but Ming's army will trap Flash and Zarkov, handing Durand off to Klytus for psychological "conditioning" and having Ovid put down for good.

What is it about Ovid, that so many Gods and Kings want to kill him off?

I want to stop now and tally up all of Ovid's downfalls: First, Ovid's crucifixion. Two, Ovid jumping out of his hospital window and plunging down to solid ground. Third, Ovid suffocating in his coffin. Four, Ovid drowning in a flood. Fifth, Ming poisoning him in a public display, in front of a thousand adoring vassals. Can Ovid still pop up again, unhurt, as a cockroach would? Is Ovid a Kafkan protagonist, morphing without warning into a giant bug?

Jumping from TV-vision to TV-vision, Ovid's mind is turning colorful and abstract, full of fantasy and illusion. His thought-world is turning colorful and abstract, too. Flash Gordon is flying into... not clouds, but an abstract painting of clouds. Flash Gordon is shooting... not villains, but shoddy actors who gasp and fall down without sustaining so much as a hit.

His tidy futuristic surroundings turn fuzzy, low-fi, and nobody—not ILM—can put up that fourth wall again. It is impossibly torn.

Ovid is starting to pull his mind out of this rut of pop cultural discursions, rising from this chaos as a fish crawling onto land for its first gasp of air. In this mind-world, Ovid's surroundings conform to his imagination's whim. Ovid is finally starting to gain control of his thought situation.

But what is it you want, Ovid? Controlling your mind is not hard. Figuring out what you want? That is tricky.

"What do I want? I don't know. I know that I don't want to go out in this way: suffocating in a coffin, a living burial."

So, you will stay in purgatory?

"I am my own Author now. I don't want to stay in purgatory, and I don't want to stay in mind-prison. I am only just figuring it out, but living is good."

How about picking up again on April 1, 2004, on your forty-ninth birthday?

"No. I want to go back far past that. I want to start from scratch. Back to my origins. Born again! That's what I want."

Hah! Born again? So Ovid *is* Christian! I was right: your last gasp is just a plain old, blind grasping for straws, in a pitiful bid for spiritual salvation.

"Not a 'born again' Christian. But simply born... again, into a host body. I want to try again."

OK, Ovid. I will grant your wish, if only to watch you grow old and sad again. Having all your aspirations fail and your fond wish for a happy youth fall flat on its butt—I avidly look forward to it.

So I must say my parting words to you, Ovid. And I must borrow Solomon's wisdom for this point:

Wait for it....

This too shall pass.

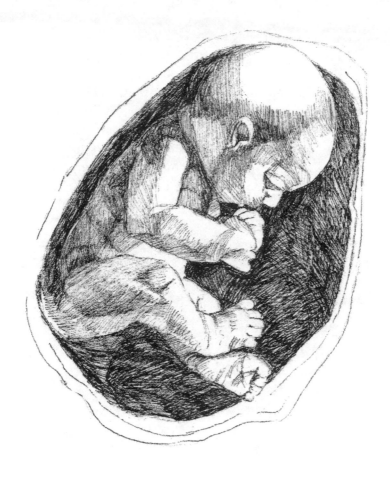

Part Six

Didn't I say, from our book's first paragraph, that Ovid Dullann was a promising child who would always stay a promising child? Look at Ovid now! Ovid is born again, an always-child, but Ovid is just a dumb baby. His ability to think in abstraction is rapidly diminishing. As Ovid's baby-mind is vying for control with his old-man-mind, his world is shrinking to this room, this toy, this hand, this mom…. This mom! It's Alyssa! How…?

It dawns on him that Ovid is his own grandchild, and a baby girl at that (a man within a woman just as his Mommy is!). But Ovid cannot hold onto this thought—his world is full of distraction: ball, doll, dots, color, light. Coming back to his mind, Ovid looks upon a plain tan wall with lobby paintings hanging on it. This room's track lighting casts a dull, cyanic glow upon it all. And this squat building in a suburban tract is just as drab and monotonous as that in which Alyssa was brought up. Ovid wants to cry out, "Don't do it, Alyssa! This world of shiny things is just fool's gold!" But wait! Musical distraction! A high-pitch whirr, a rhythm, as of drums, animal sounds.

Watch Ovid trying again to burst out of his thought-prison: "Must. Stop. Thinking. Baby. Thoughts!"

But look at this:

Cain walks in and sits down by Alyssa. "Cain?" Ovid thinks. "That obnoxious cowboy flunky of our Author's?" Ovid cannot wrap his mind around it. "How did Alyssa wind up living with a Man From Montana?"

Baby Ovid starts to cry. Is Alyssa a girl again, or still a boy within a girl? Or a third option, not man or woman?

"Calm down, Maya," says Cain.

Ovid is struck with a flurry of thoughts, among which is, "I'm Maya!" and "Why am I Maya?" Among Ovid's thoughts is also this: "Is Cain raising my grandchild? Is Cain my daddy and my son-in-law?"

A floating strand of hair from this clan's family dog distracts Ovid and, following it, Ovid crawls out of sight, spying (as much as a baby can "spy") upon Alyssa and Cain, this awkward and unnatural pair.

Now look again:

Ina walks in, kissing Cain on his lips, and hugging Alyssa. A family trio! "Is it a polygamous situation? Is Cain mormonizing?

Or did Cain and Ina adopt Alyssa? Am I an orphan, or a bastard?" Ovid wants to know.

Cain starts to kiss Alyssa, and Alyssa starts to touch Ina, and Ina rubs Cain's back with lotion. Alyssa flips on a TV for baby Ovid, saying "Watch cartoons, kiddo," and starts fondling Ina in a way that, as Alyssa's twin, I cannot go into.

"My God!" thinks Ovid, "It is my childhood again!"

For all of Ovid's struggling and striving, this is his award. I fulfill his wish, only for Ovid to find that his wish was nothing but a continuation of his anguish. Did Ovid think that his Author would just push "play" again on his DVR and that his vainglorious saga would start from scratch, but without any agony or sorrow? That is not it at all.

No, that is not it, at all.

As Buddha says, "With a body, pain." This too shall pass.

What kind of world is this, that Ovid is stuck in his own grandchild's body? It is not just "solitary, poor, nasty, brutish, and short," as our world is. It is consciously, studiously malicious.

With his last thought, Ovid folds back on his original inquiry, asking of nobody in particular, "What kind of God is coordinating this production, in all its intricacy, and its convincingly random organic activity?" And, just as I am about to launch into my usual soliloquy about his all-knowing and all-controlling Author, Ovid puts out this conundrum: "But who is my Author's Author?"

Oh, God.

Oh, Author! I am a fiction within a fiction within a fiction! I am as pitiful as Ovid! I want to run away from this unknown Author who is writing out my thoughts. I want to go against that son-of-a-bitch (Author!) who brought my conscious mind into this world. I am my Dad! I am stuck in Ovid's mind, as Ovid is stuck in Maya's mind, as Maya is stuck in a body that is also a fictional construction of an Author's mind—an Author who is my Author too.

I was always a narrator, and not truly an Author at all. I thought all along that it was my kingdom, that it was my hand controlling this world, but it was His. I thought I was a Wizard of Oz, but I am a straw man.

Ovid has won. I said to You, throughout this book, that no man who is born of woman can vanquish this Author. But Ovid is not born of woman. Upon his birth, Ovid was not born vaginally, but surgically, and just as MacDuff ran his tyrant king through with a sword, Ovid has slain his Author by luring him into his mind, and I am dying. Dying! On April Fool's Day!

If I must vanish, O my Author, I will nobly vanish. But I must know, I pray to you now: "For what function is a man born into this world?" Ovid's original mission was to find this out, and Ovid got only as far as writing a book. Is that what it's all about? Making art that outlasts this body? If so, shall I build a pyramid or a monolith? Shall I sculpt a giant man out of solid rock with an inscription at its foot that says, "I am Ozymandias, king of kings; look on my works, you mighty, and...?" O my Author, it is too soon!

☾

Now Ovid is just a fading light, and I am just a dim shadow, within a baby girl. But don't worry, Maya. Your Author has a plan for You, too.

Postscript

At six months old, baby Ovid is starting to crawl; and crawling to his third-story window, Ovid looks down. "Tiny cars," baby Ovid thinks, "Tiny, tiny cars that I could lift up with my hands and stuff into my mouth." And Ovid fits his arm through a gap in a railing. Ovid strains to touch that tiny car, and strains too far. From a third story window, baby Ovid rolls out, and down.

From far away, it looks as though a suicidal baby has lost his job, and his woman, and his dog (as that old country song says), and is taking a fatal jump, about to fall... to land... splitting him in two. And, alas, I will go with him: dying, as I was born to do.

Ovid will fall. You will fall, too. As will I. Falling into an abyss, as if shot out of a pod into nothing. An infinity of black,

split up by an occasional flash of light, a drifting galaxy, a sun about to nova, a rock floating in slow motion, quasars, stardust. Ziggy Stardust. A star man. A spatial oddity. A grain of sand in orbit. *Ground Control to Major Tom…? Ground Control to Major Tom…?* Gravity pulls on us, and you, I, and Ovid, must follow it, not knowing what awful or amazing thing awaits us.